COME THE VINTAGE

Ryan's father had left her a half share of his prosperous vine-growing business, and the other half to a man she had never heard of, a Frenchman named Alain de Beaunes – on condition that they married each other. So, for the sake of the business, they married, neither caring anything for the other. Where did they go from there?

COME THE VINTAGE

by

ANNE MATHER

MILLS & BOON LIMITED
17-19 FOLEY STREET
LONDON W1A 1DR

First published 1975
This edition 1975

© *Anne Mather 1975*

ISBN 0 263 71822 4

Made and Printed in Great Britain by
Cox & Wyman Ltd, London, Reading
and Fakenham

CHAPTER ONE

A FINE grey drizzle filtered down through the bare branches of the trees and dampened the shoulders of the few mourners gathered about the open grave. It was a fitting day for a funeral. Since early morning, clouds had hung low over the valley, and a chill wind brought the breath of snow from the Jurals not far away. The cemetery was erected on the hillside, above the village, and the weathered gravestones of its occupants were streaked with rain and sodden leaves. Autumn had come late to the valley, but it was here now, and Ryan shivered in spite of her warm coat and trousers.

She had her arms wrapped closely about her as if to ward off the chill which came as much from within as without. Despite the solemnity of the occasion, the brass-handled coffin lying in its six feet of earth, the sombrely clad group around her, she found it all very hard to believe. Was it possible that in the space of four short weeks her whole life could change so dramatically that she no longer recognized it as being her life?

Four weeks ago when Aunt Maggie died, her grief had been tempered by the letter her aunt had left. The letter, which had given her her father's address and begged her to go and see him. Since Ryan's mother had died five years before, Aunt Maggie had talked often about her father, softening the bitterness she had always felt towards him on her mother's behalf. Aunt Maggie had tried to make her see that Pierre Ferrier had not been wholly to blame for the break-up of her parents' marriage, there had been faults on both sides; most particularly her mother's refusal to return with him to France.

Ryan had thought for a long time before contacting

her father. It was ten years since she had seen him, and then she had been a mere child of some nine years, totally incapable of judging what manner of man he might be. But the realization that with the death of her aunt she was alone in the world had persuaded her to send him a letter advising him of her aunt's death. His reply had been reassuringly swift, in the form of an invitation, urging her to give up her job as an assistant librarian in a small south coast town, and join him at Bellaise in the valley of a tributary of the River Rhone. The Ferrier vineyards were there, her father's inheritance, and he wished for her to share his life.

In the days that followed Ryan had pondered his suggestion. Although her father was French, she was not, and although she spoke the language she had been taught at school, not by experience. It was a big step, expecting her to give up everything she had known and cared about and leave England to make her life in a strange country.

She had discussed the matter at length with her aunt's solicitor, and it was this which had finally decided her to go. Her aunt's house was rented, she was told, and the owners required possession as soon as possible. What little money her aunt had left would barely pay the funeral expenses, and her own earnings would scarcely enable her to rent a flat in these inflationary days. If she remained in England, she would need to find a room in a boarding house, and that prospect had filled her with dismay.

The priest's voice was droning on and Ryan felt a certain dryness in her throat. Could anyone have foreseen that fate would play such cruel games with her? If she had known her father would die of a heart attack within four days of her arrival in France, would she then have come? Would she have risked so much for four short days?

She did not know. Meeting her father again after all the years had been a bitter-sweet experience. He had

6

seemed so much older than she had expected, thin and grey-cheeked, nothing like the dark-haired man she could vaguely remember. But of course, she had been unaware of his illness . . .

His delight in seeing her had dispelled a little of the grief she had felt at the death of her aunt. Although there were things between them which could never be erased, they had both felt an immediate affinity which time and experience would have strengthened. It was eight years since her mother had divorced her French husband, but he had not married again. Ryan was his only offspring. But she had had no idea of his intentions . . .

She raised her eyes now and looked across the yawning chasm of the grave to the man standing alone at the opposite side. Alain de Beaunes – her father's partner, though she had been unaware he had a partner until she met the man.

As his curious tawny eyes lifted to meet hers, she quickly looked away. There were things which had been said between them that morning which she did not want to have to remember until she was forced to do so. Even so, that did not prevent her from shivering at the recollection of the scene which had taken place.

The priest was sprinkling soil down on to the coffin. It echoed hollowly as it fell on the hard surface, and Ryan wondered morbidly how long it would take to rot in this damp ground. Not long. She took an involuntary step backward. For a moment she felt dizzy, probably because she had had nothing to eat since morning, and she had a horror of pitching forward into the grave.

The short service appeared to be over. The priest had moved from his position and was now talking in undertones to Alain de Beaunes. Ryan couldn't help looking at them wondering what they were discussing so earnestly. Was it to do with her? Her gaze flickered over the surplice-clad figure of Abbé Maurice. Thin and slight, the frailty of his appearance was accentuated by the tall

7

powerful frame of the man standing beside him, his head stooped to listen to what the priest was saying. Alain de Beaunes was a big man. He in no way resembled the man who had been his partner, Ryan's father. Ryan had felt an aversion to him on sight, due no doubt to the bluntness of his manner, the lack of common politeness in his treatment of her. Looking at him now, noting the strong, Slavic features, the thick neck and square powerful shoulders, the long, muscular legs moulded against his trousers by the pressure of the wind, she felt totally incapable of facing what was to come. She didn't know why he intimidated her so, but he did, and she turned her attention to his shabby overcoat and carelessly blown hair in an attempt to disparage her fears. He was not a handsome man, nor yet a particularly young one. She guessed him to be in his early forties, and although some women might find his harshly carved features and heavy-lidded eyes attractive, she was repelled by him. His hair had a generous sprinkling of grey, she noticed with satisfaction, but as it had once been very fair it had now acquired the ash-blond appearance much sought after by women in expensive hair salons. Nevertheless, she regarded him as a peasant, and found no pleasure in his company. She had resented her father's obvious dependence on him, the way he had deferred to the younger man in all things, and now that her father was dead she resented his authority over her.

But what authority was it? She scuffed her boot impatiently against the stony earth. None that she could actually lay her finger on, and yet he controlled her future as surely as if her father had left her in his care. Why had her father done such a thing? Why had he made the situation so impossible? Was it a final gesture against his dead wife? She didn't know. All she knew was that she was in the most ignominious position of her life.

Abbé Maurice was approaching her now, shaking his

grey head at the leaden skies. 'The day is weeping, Ryan,' he said in his own language. 'Come – let us get back to the warmth of our firesides.'

Ryan forced a smile and allowed him to take her arm and lead her away from the graveside. She was conscious of Alain de Beaunes following them, and behind him the few villagers who had turned out to see her father laid to rest. A dusty black station wagon waited on the gravelled track which wound through the cemetery, and as they neared it Alain de Beaunes went ahead to open the doors. His shabby overcoat flapped in the wind and his dark suit had seen better days, and yet he had an arrogance which defied anyone to underestimate him.

Avoiding his eyes, Ryan climbed into the back of the station wagon. Abbé Maurice sat in the front and de Beaunes took his place behind the wheel. The black-clad villagers would make their own way to their homes and Ryan looked back only once as the vehicle bumped away down the track. Already the grave-digger was filling in the space above the coffin and she turned back quickly, her throat tightening in the way it had done so many times these last days.

The Abbé and de Beaunes were talking together and she tried to interpret what they were saying. But they spoke swiftly and in undertones and she gave up after a while and allowed her own thoughts to fill her head.

What was she going to do? Her whole being shrank away from the future her father had mapped out for her, and yet she was honest enough to know that it had to be considered in all its aspects. That was the French half of her, she supposed, the practical working of a French mind which far from being governed by emotion as was sometimes supposed could take a situation and analyse it objectively, realistically.

They were coming down the valley and she stared broodingly out of the windows. It looked a barren place, a

9

remote area where the people depended so much upon one another for their livelihood. The broad flatness at the base of the terraces where the vines grew was threaded by the swift flowing waters of the Bajou, and tall poplars lined the river bank. The village with its grey-spired church and slate-grey roofs had only one narrow street, cobbled, and uninspiring in the rain. There were cottages lining the street, a stores, a garage, and the school, and beyond the village the road wound up again towards the weathered walls of her father's house, a rambling old building whose stone-flagged floors struck chill against bare feet. And yet it was an attractive house, a house with character, and when her father was alive, filled with warmth, too. But to consider returning there *alone* with the thin-lipped stranger who occupied the seat beside the Abbé filled her with dismay.

Alain de Beaunes stopped the station wagon at the small gate to the priest's house, and the Abbé turned to speak to her.

'Do not look so alarmed, my child,' he said gently. 'God works in curious ways. I will come and see you tomorrow when you have had a little time to assuage your grief. Be thankful you had these days with your father. He might have died without ever knowing what a beautiful young woman you have grown into.'

'Thank you.' Ryan managed a lifting of the corners of her mouth, but it was difficult. Her face felt stiff, the muscles taut, unyielding.

'God go with you, my child, and with you, Alain.' The Abbé made the sign of the cross and climbed out of the vehicle. The station wagon was put into motion again and the priest soon became a shadowy figure disappearing into the gloom of the afternoon.

Ryan pressed her shoulders back against the leather of the seat. She was trying hard not to give in to the shivering which trickled up and down her spine. Somehow she had to gather her strength to face what was to come and remember that her destiny was in her own hands. But she felt more alone now than she had done at the time of her aunt's death.

Dusk was gathering as the station wagon turned between the wooden gateposts which gave on to the cobbled yard at the back of the house. The hens which scratched a living amongst the grains of animal foodstuffs scattered near the barn had long since sought the warmth and dryness of their coops, and the sound of the rain dripping from overflowing pipes added to the melancholy air of the place. No lights gleamed from the windows of the house, there was no smell of cooking to tantalize the nostrils, it looked desolate; as desolate, Ryan thought, as she felt.

Alain de Beaunes parked the station wagon beneath the bare branches of an elm tree where in summer one could sit on the circular wooden bench which surrounded it. Ryan wondered how often her father had sat beneath this tree, smoking his pipe, and perhaps wondering about his estranged wife and daughter in England. No one would want to sit on the bench now. It was too wet, and cold, and the wind blowing down from the high mountains could pierce the most adequate clothing.

Alain de Beaunes thrust open his door and climbed out without a word, swinging open the rear door as he did so. Then he left her to walk towards the back of the house, pushing open the kitchen door and disappearing inside.

Ryan sat for a few more minutes, mutinously, delaying the moment when she must get out of the car and follow him. She saw a light appear in the kitchen window and by its harsh illumination she saw him filling a kettle with water, setting it on the stove. She took a deep breath and knew that at any moment he would appear at the door again and demand her presence. She pushed her legs over the valance and slid out, closing the door behind her.

The kitchen was large, the room where most of the eating, as well as the cooking, was done. Its ceiling was beamed and hanging from it were the inevitable strings of onions. The fireplace was wide and leaded, but its adjoining oven had been superseded by a comparatively modern gas cooker. At the moment the fire was smouldering sulkily, but Alain de Beaunes was adding fresh wood which, when it caught hold, would flare up encouragingly. A scrubbed wooden table was still set with the bread and ham which her unwilling host had supplied in lieu of lunch before leaving, but Ryan had been unable to eat a thing. The lighting in the building was electric, a modern innovation supplied by their own small generator.

Now Alain de Beaunes turned from the fire and saw her hovering in the doorway. His dark brows ascended interrogatively and then he said: 'Don't you think it's time we started talking to one another?'

He spoke in French, but Ryan chose to reply in English. She knew his English was not good, and the chances were that he would not understand her. 'After our confrontation this morning, I should have thought it was obvious that our differences outweigh all other considerations.'

His lips tightened at the deliberately chosen words, and for a moment she was afraid of what he might do. He came towards her, but when she backed away he ignored her and merely closed the kitchen door, sealing them in the gathering tension of the kitchen. Then he took off his overcoat and jacket and slung them carelessly over a chair before rolling up his sleeves. His arms were strong and muscular, darkened to a deep tan by the heat of the sun, his collar when he loosened it revealed a broad chest liberally covered with fine brown hair. This was how she had first seen him, coming in from the fields, apparently unaware of his latent sensuality. Perhaps it was this that had repelled her so, this knowledge of that earthy quality about him, the hair on his body, the thick straight hair of his head which brushed the collar of his shirt, his flesh which aroused a feeling almost of distaste within her. She was not used to men in such a raw state. She had been brought up in a house of women, and the young men she had encountered in the course of her work as a librarian had not prepared her for anyone like Alain de Beaunes.

She looked away from him and approached the fire, holding out her cold hands to the blaze. There were wooden settles beside the fire and she perched on one of these, holding herself closely. When she had first come here, a little over a week ago, she had experienced a sense almost of homecoming. The house, which had reminded her a lot of farmhouses in England, the open fires instead of central heating, the smell of home-baked bread which Berthe, her father's housekeeper, had baked in the oven adjoining the fireplace; all these things had warmed and cheered her. But now her father was dead, and she had no idea whether Berthe would return. She had gone to her family two days ago, and Ryan had not liked to question her. Besides, it wouldn't matter to her, she would soon be leaving herself . . .

The kettle began to sing and she heard Alain de Beaunes setting out cups and a jug of cream. He made tea, a habit her father had acquired during his years in England, and when it was ready he handed her a cup.

'Thank you.' She took the tea reluctantly, and he stood looking down at her with obvious impatience.

'What are you going to do?' he demanded at last.

Deciding there was no point in antagonizing him further, Ryan looked up and said, in his own language: 'You know what I am going to do, *monsieur*.'

'Do I?' His curious tawny eyes were cold.

'I explained this morning. I – I have no intention of staying here.'

'Why not?'

'*Why not?*' She almost choked over the words. '*Monsieur*, my father may have been a Frenchman, and I must accept that things are done differently in his country, but I am English! I have no intention of – of satisfying some

13

– some crazy notion my father dreamed up!'

'Why is it crazy? I would suggest it is a most sensible solution to your problems.'

Ryan unfastened her coat. Suddenly she was hot. 'Well, I'm sorry to disappoint you, but I disagree.'

Alain de Beaunes seated himself on the settle opposite, legs apart, hands hanging loosely between. For such a big man he moved sinuously, and she tried to avoid the temptation to watch him.

'Ryan,' the way he said her name was curiously alien in intonation. 'Ryan – what do you intend to do if you go back to England? You have no job, I know you have no money—'

'Oh, yes, I know you know that!'

His eyes darkened with quickly suppressed anger. 'I do not deny that I found your sudden dependence on a father you had not seen for more than ten years less than admirable, nevertheless, I am prepared to admit that your presence here brought him a certain amount of satisfaction in those last few days.'

'Am I supposed to thank you for that?' Ryan was insolent.

Ignoring her outburst, he said: 'You are young, Ryan. Very young. But as you grow older you will learn that the world can be a very cold and unfriendly place to someone with neither home nor job nor money.'

Ryan forced herself to look into the fire. 'I'll manage.'

'Will you?' She was conscious of his eyes upon her. 'Tell me, please, how do you intend getting back to England? As I understood the situation, your father told me you had used most of what you possessed to get here.'

Ryan's head jerked round. 'I—' She broke off with a little gesture. 'I'll borrow the money.'

'From whom?'

'You're not offering, I suppose?'

'Oh, no.' He shook his head.

Ryan pressed her lips together. 'I – I'll speak to Abbé Maurice—'

'Abbé Maurice has barely enough to live on. Priests do not earn comfortable salaries here. They do not live in detached houses, and buy new cars every year.'

Ryan stared at him. 'You seem to know a lot about it,' she retorted sarcastically.

'I have been in England. I have read books. I am not entirely the barbarian you would like to think I am.'

Ryan flushed then, but the heat of the fire could be held responsible for the darkening of colour in her cheeks. 'I'll manage somehow,' she insisted.

Alain de Beaunes shrugged. He got up and went to a cupboard and took out a bottle of red wine. He uncorked the bottle, found a glass, and brought them both back to his seat near the fire. Pouring some of the ruby liquid into the glass, he held it up to the light for a moment, examining it intently, before nodding his satisfaction at its clarity. Then he raised the glass to his lips and drank some of the wine. Its bouquet drifted across to Ryan, rich and fruity, his lips reddened for a moment before he licked them clean.

When he lowered his glass, he looked again at Ryan. 'This wine has matured with age, little one, as all things do. Once it was rough and bitter – as you are. Now it is rich and full-bodied.'

'Spare me your similes, *monsieur*.' Ryan shifted irritably. 'I should have never have come here. I should never have written to my father.'

'And do you think if you had not written to your father that this situation would not have arisen? I assure you, it would.'

'What do you mean?'

'Your father did not make his will during these few days that you have been in France. His decision was made some time ago.'

'And you knew of it?' Ryan was aghast.

Alain de Beaunes hesitated. 'Not – entirely, no.'

Ryan shook her head. 'And you believe that – that had my aunt still been alive – and I still been living in England – that – that my father would have made the same stipulation?'

'I know he would.'

Ryan got unsteadily to her feet and walked dazedly across the room. 'But – why? Why?'

'It was what he wanted.'

'And you had no – objection?'

'Let us say I – did not care, one way or the other.'

Ryan felt sick. It was as much with emptiness as anything, but the nausea that filled her was equally upsetting. 'I – I can't marry you, *monsieur*,' she got out thickly. 'Please, let us say no more about it.'

Alain de Beaunes regarded her impatiently. 'There is no one in England, is there?'

'Of course not.'

'Then what is your objection?'

'I've explained—'

'All you have said is that you cannot marry me. No – that you *would* not marry me! That you believe I took advantage of your father in accepting a partnership with him when I had nothing to offer but my strength.'

Ryan took a deep breath. 'Half the vineyard is yours, *monsieur*. Is that not enough for you?'

'And half – should you refuse to accept your share – will belong to Gaston Aubert, your father's greatest rival. Is that what you want, English miss?'

'Of course it's not what I want.' Ryan shifted restlessly from one foot to the other. 'But your acceptance of your share does not involve entering into a marriage with a – with someone you – you—'

'Despise?' He finished the sentence for her. 'Oh, yes, I am aware of your aversion for me, *mademoiselle*. However, your feelings do not enter into it so far as I am concerned. I am concerned only for the vineyard. I know your father depended on you understanding his feelings in this.'

'Then why did he do it?' she burst out hotly.

Alain de Beaunes finished his wine and rose to his feet, towering over her. She was quite a tall girl, but he was so much bigger, so much broader, that he dwarfed her.

'You are either being very obtuse, or very stupid,' he said coldly. 'Consider the situation. Whether you like it or not, your father needed me. He was not strong. He had been ill for many years. Doctors had warned him he should give up working altogether. But this he could not do. The vineyard was his inheritance, it was his *life*. Your mother, so he said, could not accept this. She was a cold, foolish woman, more fitted to afternoon bridge clubs than working in the fields. Oh—' this as she would have protested, '—this is my interpretation, not his. Your father always spoke most regretfully about your mother. So – this is the position. When your father knows he is dying, what is he to do? No matter what you may have been told, he never stopped thinking about you. He used to talk to me of his little girl, and of how, some day, he hoped you would come to the valley and share his delight in cultivating the vines to make some of the finest wines of the district. But, being the man he is, he feels loyalty to me. He cannot leave me the vineyard, that would not be right. You are his flesh and blood, his heir. But he would not – he *could* not hand it to someone who knew nothing of the vine, of the grape, someone who might sell – to the Auberts.' He shrugged. 'He is still very much a Frenchman, your father. He knows that the marriage of convenience is still the most successful marriage there is. He tries to – manipulate us, no?'

Ryan had listened to him in silence, but now she turned away. 'You cannot manipulate people, *monsieur*.'

'Can you not?' Alain de Beaunes voice contained a trace of mockery. 'So you intend to leave?'

'Of course.' She swung round on him angrily. 'Did you

think that what you have just told me would change my mind?'

He ran his long fingers through the heavy straightness of his hair. 'I thought it might have done,' he conceded.

'Well, it hasn't.' Ryan's lips moved tremulously. 'I – I'm sorry, of course. I understand your difficulties—'

'*You!* You understand nothing!' His voice was harsh now.

'I do not wish to enter into another argument with you, *monsieur*—'

'Do you not?' His lips twisted. 'Then that is unfortunate, because I cannot stand by and watch you destroy everything your father and his father before him ever worked for without making some effort to show you how selfish you are being.'

'I didn't ask for a share of the vineyard!'

'Didn't you?' He put his hands on his hips. 'Then why did you come here?'

'I came to see my father.' Ryan was trembling now. 'And – and in any case, you said yourself, it would have made no difference—'

Alain de Beaunes swung away from her as though afraid if he remained near her he would strike her. Ryan watched him nervously, and then said: 'Why couldn't he have left me half the vineyard without that condition?'

'And what would you have done then?'

Ryan shrugged. 'I – I don't know.'

Alain turned to face her. 'Shall I tell you? You would have sold it. Without ever coming here to see it for yourself.'

'You don't know that!' she exclaimed.

'Don't I?' His lips curled. 'I think I do. I think your father knew you were half your mother's daughter, after all.'

'Don't you dare slander my mother!'

'Why not? Don't you think she treated your father

abominably?'

Ryan's breathing was swift and shallow. 'You know nothing about it.'

'Don't I?' he mocked again. 'I know what your father told me. He was a sick man before he returned to France.'

Ryan stared at him unbelievingly. 'Wh-what are you saying?'

'Don't you know? Didn't your mother tell you? Your father developed a heart condition almost two years before he left England.'

'*No!*'

'It's the truth. And the climate did not help. Wet summers, cold winters; he was a prey to bronchial complaints, complaints which weakened the muscles of his heart.'

'I don't believe you.'

Ryan couldn't allow herself to believe him. Her mother could not have permitted her father, a sick man, to return to France alone knowing that he might die at any time!

Alain hunched his shoulders. 'Nevertheless, it is the truth,' he asserted firmly. 'I am sorry if it destroys the image you have of your mother, but quite frankly your father's last wishes are all that concern me.'

Ryan sought one of the wooden chairs that flanked the kitchen table, and sat down rather heavily. Her legs no longer felt strong enough to support her, and the sickness she had felt turned to a dull throbbing in her temples. Could it be true? Could it be proved? Surely Alain de Beaunes would not risk telling her something like this knowing that her father's doctor could refute it if it was not true.

She looked up at him unsteadily, her pale cheeks and hollowed eyes eloquent of the shock she had suffered. 'I – I never knew.'

'I believe you.' His tone was less aggressive, but without sympathy.

Ryan shook her head helplessly. 'How – how could she?'

'That's what I asked myself, many times.'

Ryan pressed her palms together. 'I – I need time to think.'

'About what?'

She glanced up at him piteously. 'You know about what.'

He shrugged and turned away. 'I have things to do. Life goes on, even in the face of death. You'll let me know your decision, of course.' Sarcasm had crept in to his tones.

Ryan closed her eyes against the sight of him. Then she opened them again and said: 'I – I have to do it, don't I?'

'That's for you to decide.'

'No, it's not.' She gazed at him desperately. 'What – what did you mean by – by a marriage of convenience?'

'Exactly what it says. I have no interest in a child, *mademoiselle*.'

Her cheeks burned. 'I'm not a child, or the situation would not arise.'

'Maybe not in years, but in experience . . .'

'And – and are you experienced, *monsieur*?'

She didn't know what made her ask the question, except that she sensed he would have no small knowledge of her sex. He regarded her disconcertingly for a while, and then said: 'As much as any man who has already had one wife.'

Ryan gasped. 'You – you have a wife, *monsieur*?'

'I *had*,' he corrected expressionlessly. 'My wife died almost ten years ago.'

'Almost ten years ago!' Ryan found it hard to take in. Ten years ago she had been a child . . .

'I am forty years of age, *mademoiselle*. Old enough to be your father, I admit. Perhaps you had better regard

20

our relationship in that light. With luck, you could be a widow before you are my age.'

Ryan sucked in her breath on a sob. 'Don't say such things!'

'No?' He moved his shoulders indifferently. 'Perhaps not. Perhaps I will live my three score years and ten. Perhaps even a little more. Who knows? A life sentence, *mademoiselle*, is it not? I am sorry, but I did not make the rules. Your father did that.'

CHAPTER TWO

RYAN's room was at the head of the twisting flight of stairs which led to the upper reaches of the house. It was not a large room and towards the eaves the ceiling sloped a little, but it was a comfortable room and when she had first seen it, Ryan had been delighted with it. The uneven floorboards were covered with fluffy wool rugs, the bedspread was a rich folkweave, and the curtains were patterned with sprigs of lilac. If the furniture – the iron-posted bedstead, the heavy tallboy, the mahogany wardrobe and dressing table, were a little outdated, they nevertheless shone from frequent polishings, and the room smelt sweetly of freshly laundered sheets and beeswax.

On the morning following her father's funeral, Ryan stood by the window of her room, looking down the sweeping length of the valley. She could see the river, the terraced hillside, the houses huddled at its base, the reaching spire of the church of St. Augustine, and the distant mountains where the snow could always find a resting place. In summer when the snows receded to the high plateau, the goatherds sought the lush pastures that had been hidden all winter long, and the air echoed with the sound of goat bells, but now it was almost time for the snow to come again and Ryan shivered at the prospect.

Still, the rain had departed and the morning was fresh and clear, if a little chill. Ryan had been dressed since the first grey fingers of light probed her bedroom curtains, but she had delayed the moment of going downstairs and confronting Alain de Beaunes. The evening before had a curiously unreal quality about it, and although she had slept almost as soon as her head touched the pillow, she had been awake early, lying staring into the darkness, trying not to feel afraid of the future.

But it was impossible for her not to do so. The idea of marrying a man she had known little more than a week was a terrifying prospect, particularly as that man inspired no confidence inside her. He was so much older, so much more experienced, so big and powerful, so much a man in every sense of the word. She had seen the broad strength of his shoulders, the hair-covered skin of his chest which narrowed to a flat stomach, the muscles bulging against the taut cloth which covered his thighs; how could she believe him when he said theirs would be a marriage of convenience only, that he had no interest in her? Once they were married, she would have no defence against him except his word.

A disturbing shivering sensation ran down her spine and into her legs. *Married!* Married to Alain de Beaunes! She would be Ryan de Beaunes; Ryan Ferrier, no longer. It was an incredible prospect!

The church bells were ringing out the hour and she glanced automatically at her watch. It was nine o'clock. She would have to go downstairs and face her future husband. She caught her breath on a gulp. If it was not so deadly serious, it would be laughable.

A slim figure in denim jeans and a chunky green sweater, her chestnut dark hair confined with an elastic band, she descended the winding staircase and reached the panelled hall. A smell of freshly ground coffee emanated from the direction of the kitchen, and Ryan's spirits rose when she thought that perhaps Berthe had returned.

But when she opened the kitchen door, it was not the plump housekeeper who was bending over the fire, but Alain de Beaunes, his tanned skin contrasting sharply with the curious lightness of his hair. Dressed in close-fitting corded pants and a thick black sweater, his trousers pushed into tall black boots, he had obviously been outside, and he exuded an aura of virile good health.

23

'Good morning, Ryan,' he greeted her easily, as though nothing had changed since the previous day. 'I was just about to bring you some coffee upstairs.'

Ryan closed the door and leaned back against it. 'That wasn't necessary,' she managed, picturing her own alarm at the image of him entering her bedroom. He would dwarf its less than generous proportions.

He shrugged, and indicated the percolator on the stove. 'Help yourself,' he directed. 'I am afraid there is no fresh bread, but perhaps tomorrow . . .'

Ryan crossed the room rather awkwardly, and reaching down a mug from the dresser poured some of the strongly flavoured liquid into it. She added cream and sugar and stood cradling the cup in her two hands, watching him adding wood to the already blazing logs. Then she licked her lips and said: 'When is Berthe coming back?'

Alain straightened and looked round at her, brushing his palms over the seat of his pants. 'Berthe is not coming back,' he replied flatly.

Ryan's eyes were wide. 'Not – coming – back?' she faltered.

'No.' Alain lifted his shoulders expressively. 'Berthe stayed because of your father. Now there is to be another mistress in the house, she has left.'

Ryan's cheeks coloured. 'But – but that's not necessary.'

'Isn't it?'

'No.' Ryan spread an expressive hand. 'Who – who will do all the cooking here – the cleaning – looking after the animals?' Then at the mocking look in his eyes, she uttered an exclamation of protest. 'Not *me*!'

'Why not you? What do you intend to do all day?'

Ryan sought for words, swallowing some of the coffee as though its bitterness might sharpen her means of retaliation. 'I – I – I'm not a housekeeper!'

'What are you, then? Or rather, what do you intend to be?'

Ryan's brows drew together. 'I – I'm a librarian—'

'There are no libraries in Bellaise.'

'I could do other work – other office work—'

'For whom? I know – you may take charge of the book-keeping which up till now I have dealt with myself.'

Ryan bent her head. 'You don't understand—'

'On the contrary, Ryan, it is *you* who do not understand.' He felt about in his pockets and drew out a case of narrow cheroots. He put one between his teeth, and as he lighted it with a spill from the fire, he went on: 'Let me tell you something, may I?' He did not wait for her acquiescence, but continued: 'You have a lot to learn, Ryan. Oh, I know your father has shown you the vineyards, taken you down to the cellars, and introduced you to the men who work for us. But as yet, you know nothing of our life here. Ours is a small vineyard. We produce less than two hundred cases of wine every year. But we like to think that what we do produce is good, very good. Our wine is comparatively unknown as yet. It is drunk locally, in the hotels and restaurants of the tourist resorts, but we do not make a lot of money. We do not compare to the great wine-producing chateaux of Bordeaux and Burgundy. In consequence, our life is quite simple. We do not waste money employing housekeepers when the mistress of the house is perfectly capable of running her own establishment, do I make myself clear?'

'But I've never – I wouldn't know how—'

'You will learn. I will employ a young girl from the village to help you with the heavy tasks, but you will find there is reward in knowing yourself capable of managing alone.'

Ryan finished her coffee and put the mug down heavily on the draining board. 'You have it all worked out, haven't you?' she demanded bitterly. 'When did you tell Berthe she would no longer be needed? As soon as my father was dead? Were you so sure I'd agree to your outrageous plans?'

'They were not *my* plans, *mademoiselle*,' he retorted, and his voice had cooled perceptibly. 'I suggest you stop feeling sorry for yourself and start appreciating your good fortune!'

'The good fortune of marrying you, *monsieur*?' she taunted him insolently, and then felt an inward thrill of fear at the menacing darkening of his tawny eyes.

'Have a care, little one,' he said chillingly. 'Once we are man and wife I will have certain rights where you are concerned. Do not tempt me to exert them.'

Ryan's cheeks flamed now. 'But you said—'

'There are other rights beside the conjugal ones,' he retorted swiftly. Then he made an impatient gesture. 'But this is getting us nowhere. I suggest we stop this bickering and begin accepting that for both of us there will have to be – adjustments.'

'Adjustments?' Ryan felt stupidly near to tears. She knew whose the greater adjustment would be. Schooling her features, she nodded. 'All right, all right. I suppose I have no choice, as I'm to be confined here . . .'

'In what way confined?' His voice was dangerously quiet.

Ryan spread her hands, unconsciously revealing her likeness to her father. 'What else is there for me to do? There are no buses here. No trains that I can see. I can hardly walk to the nearest town, can I, and the village isn't exactly huge!'

'You don't drive?' It was more of a statement than a question. 'No? Then I will teach you. There are two vehicles here – the station wagon, and a Landrover. You are welcome to use either of those when you have become proficient. Anciens is only twenty kilometres away. There are shops there, and a cinema. And a library, too, should you require one.' This last was said with a reversion to his earlier mockery, but Ryan chose to ignore it.

'Thank you.'

He inclined his head. 'It is nothing. And now I suggest

26

you help yourself to something to eat. Fatigue follows swiftly on the heels of malnutrition.'

Ryan shook her head. 'I'm not hungry.'

'You will be before the morning is over. I suggest you spend the time exploring your domain. The Abbé Maurice will no doubt join us for lunch. Perhaps you should be considering what you are going to offer him.'

Ryan stared at him in horror. 'You – expect me to provide a meal?'

Alain walked towards the kitchen door and picked up a black leather coat he had thrown ready for use over the back of a chair. 'I have to go into Bellaise to see Gilbert Chauvin. I expect to be back soon after one o'clock. You will find the larder is well stocked, and there is a deep-freeze in the storeroom. Berthe was a careful housekeeper. I do not think you will be disappointed. Do not trouble to enter the cellar. I myself will choose the wine when I return.'

'But—' Ryan took a step towards him. 'I mean, I've never served a meal before!'

Alain opened the door, and stood regarding her with scarcely-concealed amusement. 'There is always a first time for everything, little one. *Adieu* – and good luck!'

Ryan stood motionless as the door closed behind him, and after a few moments she heard the station wagon's engine roar to life. She hurried to the window as the tyres crunched over the cobbles of the yard, but he did not turn to look at her as the vehicle drove between the gateposts and disappeared down the track towards the village.

She told herself she was glad to see him go, but with his departure the house seemed suddenly very empty, and very isolated. For a girl who all her life had been spared the drudgery of housework, it seemed there was a tremendous amount to learn, and she hadn't the first idea where to start.

Remembering that someone had once told her that the best way to clean a house was from the top down, she looked doubtfully towards the door which led into the hall. The bedrooms, she supposed, were the place she should begin. But where was Alain de Beaunes' bedroom, and was she expected to make his bed?

Shaking her head, as if to shake away the sense of bewilderment and confusion that filled it, she walked purposefully into the hall and up the stairs. The first landing, where her room was situated, presented what seemed to be an alarming amount of doors to her inexperienced eye. But after discovering broom cupboards, and airing cupboards, and renewing her acquaintance with the rather antiquated bathroom, she discovered that there were only four bedrooms to cope with. The room which had been her father's offered an air of melancholy which she was little prepared to bear in her emotional state, and she quickly closed the door again, promising herself that she would go through his things fully when time had dulled perception. Apart from her own room, there only were two other rooms, one of which was dust-sheeted, and the other was Alain de Beaunes'.

She hesitated before entering his bedroom, but then pushed away her feelings of distaste. After all, once they were married she would have to get used to caring for his clothes, washing his linen, making his bed. All the same, she felt somewhat of an intruder as she hung his bathrobe on the hook behind the door, straightened the tumbled pillows and smoothed the sheets of the bed. There were no pyjamas lying about, and she assumed he must have folded them away into a drawer. It was an odd thing for him to have done, but it was not up to her to question his actions.

When the bed was made and the coverlet had been neatly spread, she looked round with reluctant curiosity. What was there here to indicate what manner of man he was? A bookcase beside the bed revealed a selection of theses on viticulture, books on economics and the geology of the Rhone basin, and a couple of novels, which

Ryan herself would not have been opposed to reading. A bedside cabinet supported a lamp and an alarm clock, but she respected his privacy sufficiently not to probe into its drawers and cupboard.

The furniture matched that in her own own room, although his bed was broader and longer, and looked rather more comfortable. On impulse, she opened the wardrobe door and looked at the clothes hanging inside. There were not many, obviously Alain de Beaunes did not pay a lot of attention to keeping up with current fashions, but as she closed the door again she had to concede that in his case clothes were merely a necessary covering and not something to accentuate his masculinity. His masculinity was in no doubt.

Realizing she was wasting time, she quickly left his bedroom, made her own bed and tidied her room, and then went downstairs again.

A mewing at the kitchen door admitted the huge tortoiseshell-coloured tabby which had occupied the settle by the fire until Berthe's departure, and which Ryan had assumed belonged to her. But now the cat walked into the kitchen as though it owned the place, and ignoring Ryan completely took up its former position on the settle. Although piqued at its treatment of her, Ryan was almost glad of its company, and there was something reassuring about knowing it was there, relaxed and uncaring, licking its paws.

Her distraction had cost more time and her eyes sought the clock on the mantelshelf with some alarm. It was half past ten already. How long did meat take to cook, and what on earth was she to give them for lunch?

As she pushed the dirty dishes from the table into the sink, she reflected that Alain at least had had breakfast that morning. There was the sweet smell of conserve on his knife, and a thick slice had been cut from the crusty loaf that still resided on the table. A quick look round revealed a bread bin, and she stuffed the remains of the

29

loaf inside, and closed the lid over the curls of butter in their dish. As she did so her own stomach gave a knowing little rumble, and she sighed. She ought to have something to eat. But time was precious, and she steeled herself against hunger.

The storeroom adjoined the kitchen. She had been in there once with Berthe and seen the sacks of salt and flour, the bins containing sugar and dried fruit, only then she had never dreamt that in so short a time she would have charge of the household.

The freezer revealed an impressive array of meat and vegetables. Obviously Berthe had frozen a store of greens for the coming winter, as well as bottling jams and chutneys and preserved fruits. It was alarming for Ryan to imagine herself coping so efficiently. She felt sure she would never do it.

Abandoning any ideas of producing a thoroughly continental meal such as Berthe might have provided, she took some steaks from the freezer and a jar of apricots in syrup from the shelf. The meat would need some time to thaw, and she put it on a plate on the draining board while she made an inspection of the kitchen cupboards. When the fire needed more logs, she smiled as the cat protested at the sparks which flew when she put on more wood.

With the dishes washed and draining, and the table clear for the first time since Berthe's departure, Ryan began to feel she was making progress. As well as the huge kitchen, there were three other downstairs rooms, and she decided to inspect these, too. There was a dining-room, which was seldom if ever used, a parlour for sitting, which was treated with respect, and which Ryan privately thought was quite hideous with its stiff-backed chairs and antimacassars, fiddly little tables and unlikely ornaments, and the study which had been used equally by her father and Alain de Beaunes.

The study was obviously the most favoured room of

the house. Its worn leather armchairs bore witness to frequent use, and it had a comfortable untidiness that went well with its atmosphere of pipe tobacco and good wine. Papers were strewn over the wide top of the desk, and the typewriter which was pushed to one side must have been a prototype of its kind. Ryan put in a sliver of scrap paper and pressed the keys and was pleasantly surprised at the result.

She sat in the chair behind the desk and studied the vintage charts which had been framed and hung on the wall opposite. The Ferrier vineyards were obviously improving, and the charts for the past five years showed a steady rise in ratings. She felt a stirring of compassion for her father that he should have died when things were going so well. But side by side with the Ferrier charts hung those for the Aubert vineyards. Their ratings were improving also, and seemed to prove that Alain de Beaunes had not been exaggerating when he spoke of her father's rivalry with such forcefulness.

The emptiness in her stomach eventually reminded her that it was time she was preparing the meal. She could make herself some coffee while the steaks grilled, she thought, and *sauter* the vegetables for quickness.

But a shock awaited her when she returned to the kitchen. The huge tabby was licking her paws on the draining board, and the plate on which she had laid the steaks was empty.

Ryan was horrified. 'Oh, *cat*!' she exclaimed angrily, lifting the creature and dropping her unceremoniously on to the floor. 'Oh, what am I going to do now?'

Knowing she had no time to ponder, she went back into the storeroom and took three more steaks from the freezer. Their coldness clung to her fingers and without stopping to consider the advisability of such a course, she plunged them into hot water, thawing them quickly. By the time the Abbé Maurice came tapping his walking stick at the kitchen door, the meat was under the grill and

31

potatoes were frying appetizingly in the pan.

The old priest came in smiling warmly, obviously impressed by her activity. 'I see you are going to make a good housekeeper, my child,' he pronounced, sniffing the air appreciatively. 'Alain has invited me for lunch. I trust that will not inconvenience you.'

'Oh, no!' Ryan's cheeks were flushed from the heat of the stove, but she felt rather sick inside. She had still had nothing to eat, and her exertions were beginning to tell. 'Won't you sit down, Father? Can I offer you something? Some coffee – or tea?'

The old priest was breathing rather heavily, and he sat down with obvious relief. 'No, nothing just now, child,' he refused politely, taking off his hat. 'My, my,' he patted his chest, 'that walk up from the village gets steeper, I think.'

'You've walked?' Ryan was astonished. She hadn't heard a car, but she had just assumed he had used one.

'But of course. The exercise does me good. I must say, though, that after one of Berthe's good lunches, I could not always walk back, even though it is downhill,' he chuckled.

Ryan turned back to the stove. His words were rather unfortunate in the circumstances, but he was not to know that. And after all, steak and tomatoes and chips, followed by apricots and icecream, was not such a frugal repast. Perhaps she should have opened a tin of soup. She shrugged. Another day. Alain could think himself lucky he was getting any meal at all.

The station wagon roared into the yard about five minutes later, and Alain came in bringing a breath of cold frosty air with him. In his absence she had forgotten the overwhelming domination of his presence, and the penetration of those tawny cat's eyes. He greeted the priest warmly, exchanged a glance with Ryan, and then bent to the cat who had leapt from her perch to rub herself lovingly against his booted legs.

'Hey, Tabithe!' he chided gently, his deep voice acquiring a disturbing tenderness Ryan had never heard before. 'So you came back, did you? Have you been keeping our mistress company?'

Ryan lifted the potatoes into a serving dish, her hands trembling slightly. She was tempted to tell him exactly what kind of company the beastly creature had provided, but to do so would embarrass the Abbé, and she had no quarrel with him. All the same, she felt a faint resentment that her overtures towards the animal had been ignored, while Alain had only to appear for her to be caressing his legs with her sinuous body. But of course, she thought impatiently, the cat was a female, and had all the usual attraction towards the male. Obviously the creature did not regard the Abbé Maurice in his flowing robes in quite the same light.

The steak looked reassuringly good when it was served with sprigs of parsley, and Alain, who had been down to the cellar below the storeroom to fetch a bottle of wine for their delectation, stopped what he was doing to compliment her on its presentation. After a moment's hesitation, she had decided to serve the meal in the kitchen, and obviously she had done the right thing. Had she not felt so unwell, she would have been almost satisfied with her morning's work. However, the wine which Alain had uncorked and poured into her glass served to revive her.

'Ah, but this is good,' essayed the priest, nodding as he inhaled its bouquet. 'What is it, Alain? Not the '68 or the '69? It cannot be the '66. No, I think perhaps it is a Beaujolais . . .'

Alain smiled, taking his seat at the head of the table, his fingers hiding the label on the bottle in his hand. 'How astute, Father,' he murmured humorously. He partially withdrew his fingers. 'See – I will not tease you. It is from the Vosne-Romanée. But can you guess which it is?'

Abbé Maurice picked up the glass and inhaled again,

his brows drawing together in perplexity. 'You know I am no expert, Alain. A Burgundy is a Burgundy. I know what I like, and that is about all.'

Alain set the bottle down. 'It is the Richebourg, see? The '61. A very special case which Ryan's father had laid down for very special occasions.'

The priest surveyed them both expectantly. 'And this is such an occasion, Alain?'

Alain's eyes sought Ryan's, but she looked away, unable to contemplate what he was about to say. 'It is a special occasion, Father,' he agreed. 'Ryan and I are to be married, as soon as it can be arranged. Is that not so, Ryan?'

He was challenging her now. It was the moment of truth, and she was not prepared for it. 'I – yes. Yes, I suppose so.'

The old Abbé beamed. 'I could not be more pleased.' He pushed back his chair and rose to his feet. 'This calls for a toast, in this most excellent wine of the Côte de Nuits. I wish you every happiness, my children, and I drink to your future together.'

The priest insisted that they join in the toast, and he patted Alain on the shoulder and told Ryan that her father would have been so happy had he been alive to see this day. Alain had been like a son to him, he said, and it was always her father's dearest wish that his two loved ones should meet.

Ryan couldn't help thinking that had her father still been alive, this day would not have occurred. She wondered how much the priest had known of her father's affairs, of the terms of his will, and decided he had probably been a witness to it. He obviously shared her father's and Alain's belief that marriage should first and foremost be treated as a business arrangement, but the cold-bloodedness of it, the calculating method of its inception, filled Ryan with despair.

Custom satisfied, they turned to the meal. Alain served

the priest first, then Ryan, and finally himself. If he was surprised that Ryan would accept nothing more than a small steak and half a tomato, he made no comment, and for this she was thankful. But when she cut into the meat she found to her horror that although the outer casing was brown and smelt appetizing, inside the core was still hard and frozen.

She looked up aghast to find Alain and the priest eating silently, apparently unperturbed at the rawness of the meat, but her stomach revolted. What must they be thinking of her? she thought desperately. Were neither of them going to say anything? They must know she had not thawed it before cooking. They would think her an absolute idiot!

She pushed her plate aside, and waited for one of them to speak. But they said nothing, and she suddenly felt furiously angry. She didn't want their pity, she didn't want them to pretend to enjoy something so as not to hurt her feelings. It was too galling to contemplate!

Taking a deep breath, she burst out: 'Don't eat it! It's horrible! It's raw! The cat ate the meat I thawed, and I didn't have time to thaw any more.'

Abbé Maurice lifted his head in an embarrassed way, and Alain regarded her steadily. 'Don't be silly, Ryan. I prefer my steak rare.'

'There's a difference between rare and raw!' declared Ryan vehemently.

'I tell you, it's all right.' Alain's eyes had hardened slightly.

Ryan's lips moved tremulously. 'Well, I'm not going to eat it,' she retorted, pushing back her chair and getting to her feet.

'Where do you think you are going?' demanded Alain, half rising also, but she didn't reply, she merely shook her head and walked unsteadily to the door.

Somehow she made it to her room, closing the door and sinking down on the bed, tears probing hotly at her eyes.

Her first meal and it was a disaster! She would never learned to cope as efficiently as Berthe.

The door opened on her misery and she looked up in amazement to see Alain de Beaunes blocking the doorway with his bulk. His eyes were dark and angry, and his mouth was a thin line in his tanned features. He came into the room and stood looking down at her coldly.

'What do you think you are doing?' he inquired tautly. 'Is it your practice to abandon your guest half-way through the meal?'

'He's not my guest, he's yours,' she managed, biting her lips to stop them from trembling.

'He is *our* guest,' Alain corrected her shortly. 'Stop behaving so childishly. So – the meat is not thoroughly cooked! No one expects you to produce a perfect meal at the first attempt.'

'Oh, thank you. That's very reassuring to know!' she exclaimed with heavy sarcasm.

He thrust his hands into the hip pockets of his trousers, tautening the cloth across his thighs. 'I make allowances for your immaturity, little cat. Be thankful that I do.'

Ryan turned her head away, her eyes smarting from tears suppressed. 'I don't remember inviting you into my room, *monsieur*. Aren't you supposed to knock before entering a lady's bedroom?'

The exclamation he made was half anger, half amusement. 'You are determined to challenge me, are you not, little one?' he commented quietly. Then he turned towards the door. 'Very well. You have five minutes to tidy yourself, and then you will join the good Abbé and me for dessert. Do I make myself clear?'

Ryan turned to face him protestingly. 'I don't want anything else.'

'Maybe not.' His eyes assessed her in a way that caused the blood to quicken in her veins. 'You had no breakfast, did you? In spite of what I said. Your colour is high at the moment, but underneath you are pale. It is food you require, little one. Perhaps not the steak, I admit, but maybe some soup would not come amiss, eh?'

Ryan's stomach heaved restlessly. 'There is no soup.'

'There are tins. Even I am proficient with a tin opener.' He paused in the doorway and looked back at her. 'You are all right now?'

Ryan hesitated, and then she nodded. And she was. It was true. Although he had not sympathized with her, his quiet words had restored a little of her confidence. The knowledge surprised her.

CHAPTER THREE

RYAN and Alain de Beaunes were married three weeks later in the small church of St. Augustine in the village of Bellaise. The service was conducted by the Abbé himself, and as neither Ryan nor Alain had any close family present it was a very quiet affair.

During those weeks preceding the wedding, Ryan felt herself to be living in a vacuum. The whole structure of her life had changed drastically and become slightly unreal, so that she found it hard to absorb what was going on around her. Most particularly her relationship with her future husband.

It was the time of year after the excitement of the grape harvest when a certain amount of anti-climax crept into the production of the year's vintage. The initial pressing of the grapes had been achieved, and the juice transferred to casks for fermentation. Only time would tell whether the matured wine would measure up to their expectations, and consequently Alain was often at home, working in his study, and Ryan could never completely relax when he was in the house.

He had taken her, as her father had done, down to the winery, and she had descended with him into the massive stone cellars where there were casks of wine which had been maturing for a number of years. He had seemed determined that she should learn the basic fundamentals of the business, and had spent some time explaining the various difficulties they could encounter. She had met the elderly Breton again who had worked for her father, and his father before him, and shivered in the vaultlike caverns between the rows of vats.

The Ferrier vineyards bottled their own wine, and Alain showed her the small plant. He explained how later in the process the wine would be put into bottles and corked, and then inverted in racks to collect impurities on the cork. Afterwards, he said, these corks would be removed and the bottles recorked. In making a good red wine a certain amount of the crushed flesh of the grape was left in the juice during the initial stages of fermentation, but the finished product was required to have a clarity free of all sediment.

During these almost educational tours of inspection, Ryan could almost forget the improbability of their relationship. It was only when one or other of their employees congratulated Alain on his good fortune that the truth possessed her in all its terrifying reality. During the long nights when sleep was often elusive, she lay imagining the frightening possibilities of what she was about to do. What did she really know of this man who was to be her husband? The fact that her father had cared for him and depended upon him meant little to her. The relationship between two men was vastly different from the relationship between a man and his wife. The power over her which this marriage would give Alain de Beaunes was not to be considered lightly, and she had no sure way of knowing that he would keep his word about anything.

Her only companions during those weeks before the wedding were the old priest, and Marie, the girl from the village whom Alain had employed to help her. Marie was a year older than Ryan, and her initial shyness gave way to a genuine affection for the younger girl. In her way, she understood Ryan's doubts about the marriage, although her reasons for so doing differed from Ryan's own.

To Marie, it was all so simple. Alain de Beaunes was very much a man, all the women in the village thought so, whereas Ryan was little more than a child. Naturally she was anxious that he should not be disappointed in her, self-conscious about the physical aspects of the marriage. But that was nothing to worry about. The *monsieur* was no amateur, she had heard, and she would without doubt find experience something infinitely pleasurable to gain.

Ryan supposed that compared to Marie she was child-like. Her knowledge of the opposite sex was limited to several furtive embraces on the doorstep of her aunt's house after youth club socials and the like. She had never had a steady boy-friend, preferring her own company to that of some youth who seemed to think he owed it to himself to attempt to paw her about, and whose conversation was confined to television and the latest group on the pop music scene. Her upbringing had been rather old-fashioned, but through choice rather than direction.

And Marie could not have been further from the truth with regard to her coming marriage. The physical side of that relationship was something she did not hope to gain any experience of.

Marie on the other hand had had two lovers already, and had lost count of the number of boys she had known. She found Ryan's innocence rather touching, and tried, in her friendly way, to reassure her. From time to time Ryan had seen Marie's eyes resting rather enviously on the broad shoulders and lean face of the master of the house, and had realized that a man like Alain de Beaunes would have no difficulty in finding a woman to satisfy his male appetites. The knowledge disturbed her somewhat, though she didn't know why it should. It was of no interest to her how many women he chose to make love to, and no doubt, after they were married, she would feel grateful to those other women for diverting his attention from her.

After the wedding ceremony Ryan and Alain and the priest drove back to the house.

Ryan was glad to get home and change out of the white wedding dress which Marie had insisted on lending her. As Ryan had neither the time nor the inclination to

buy a wedding dress of her own, she supposed she ought
to have been grateful to the girl for providing something
suitable for her to wear. But the slightly yellowed lace
gown, which had already been worn by several members
of Marie's family, had been made for much more voluptuous curves than Ryan possessed, and consequently it
hung on her slim shoulders and looked quite dreadful to
her eyes.

Alain wore a suit of navy blue suede which fitted his
powerful body closely. Ryan had not seen it before, and
its darkness accentuated the intense lightness of his
straight hair. White cuffs showed against tanned wrists,
liberally covered with hairs, and she felt a rekindling of
the aversion she had felt towards him when they had first
met. He was so blatantly masculine, so confident, so arro-
gantly sure of himself and of her. And why not? she asked
herself bitterly. She had done exactly as he wanted. She
chose not to remember that it was what her father had
wanted first of all.

In her room she stripped off the hated dress and looked
round for her jeans. They were not lying on the chair
where she had left them, and when she impatiently
tugged open the dressing table drawer, she found her
other clothes were missing, too.

Her brows drew together in perplexity. Marie had been
in the house when they left for the church. Had she taken
the things? Why should she? What possible use could
they be to her? No, she would never do such a thing.
Ryan was sure the girl was not a thief. So where were
they?

A startling idea sent her scurrying along the landing to
Alain's room. She could hear the sound of his voice and
the Abbé's downstairs, so she felt no anxiety when she
thrust open the door and went into his room. With trembling fingers she pulled open a drawer in his dressing
table. It revealed only socks and underwear, and she
quickly shut it again. A second drawer displayed shirts and

41

sweaters, but at the third attempt she found what she was looking for. A layer of lingerie concealed nightwear and toiletries.

She stood with her fingertips pressed to her lips, staring down at the contents of the drawer, and an awful sick sensation filled her stomach. Marie must have moved her things while they were at church. But on whose authority?

'So – what have we here?'

Ryan swung round in alarm at the unexpected sound of Alain's voice. He was standing in the doorway, leaning negligently against the jamb, but there was a coldness about his eyes which belied the mockery of his tone.

'I – I–' Ryan suddenly remembered that the best method of defence was attack. 'How – how dare you have my clothes shifted into your room?'

Alain's expression did not alter, but he looked past her to the open dressing table drawer. 'Marie must have done it,' he said evenly.

'Yes. Yes, I know. But on – on whose authority?'

Alain straightened. 'Not mine, I can assure you.'

Ryan glanced back at the drawer and as she did so saw her own reflection in the dressing table mirror. She was suddenly made aware that she was facing him in her pants and slip and little else. She crossed her arms across her rounded breasts, and shifted uncomfortably.

'I want – I want my jeans, and – and a shirt,' she stated unsteadily.

'Get them.' He walked indolently into the room, unbuttoning his jacket.

'If you'll give me five minutes—'

He turned on her then. 'For God's sake, Ryan, grow up! We are married, remember? Or have you so soon forgotten?'

'No, I haven't forgotten,' she retorted, her lips trembling. 'I remember quite well that you said that it was to be a marriage of convenience only—'

'So it is!' He stared at her with eyes filled with dislike. 'What do you expect me to do? This is my room. I have more right here than you do. Just because some foolish serving girl has taken it into her head to bring your clothes in here, it does not alter the situation between us. No doubt she expected you to be pleased. The fact that you are not is something you should take up with her, not me!'

Ryan stared at him frustratedly, continuing to shield her body with her arms. 'How – how can I get changed with you – you here?'

'I believe the usual practice is to unfasten one's clothes and take them off, and then put something else on,' he returned sardonically, taking off his jacket. 'Do you want me to demonstrate?'

'You – you wouldn't dare!' she breathed.

'Why not?' To her horror his fingers moved to the belt of his trousers. 'Have you never seen an adult male without clothes before?'

'Of course not!'

She turned abruptly away, and he uttered an impatient exclamation. 'Very well,' he said, walking towards the door, and looking back at her, 'I'll give you five minutes to find what you want, and then I'm going to get changed, right?'

Ryan nodded mutely, and the door closed behind him. With his going she flew into an agony of haste and fumbling ineptitude. Her jeans were eventually located in the wardrobe, and she tugged them on, and was fastening the buttons of a dark red shirt when he came back. He viewed her appearance critically for a few moments, and then ignoring her he began to unbutton his shirt.

'I – I'll move my things back into my own room later on,' she ventured tentatively from the doorway.

He shrugged, 'As you like,' and she closed the door quietly behind her.

In her own room, she gave a little more thought to her

appearance. She had had no intention of dressing up in anything frivolous and feminine for Alain de Beaunes' benefit, no matter what the Abbé Maurice might think, but she was totally unaware that in the casual garments she had a youthful charm and attraction that owed nothing to artifice. She had grown so used to the thick curtain of her hair which curved under at her shoulders, the slightly slanted hazel eyes and tip-tilted nose, a mouth that was wide and mobile, that she no longer appreciated the beauty which together they created.

She touched the colour in her cheeks brought there by Alain's disturbing comments. *Ryan de Beaunes!* She said the name experimentally. That was her name now. *Wife* to Alain de Beaunes, a man she had known for little more than a month. A man moreover, she was realizing, she knew next to nothing about.

Downstairs, the old Abbé was rocking himself before the blazing fire, a glass of wine resting comfortably in his hand. He looked round as Ryan entered the room, and what he saw seemed to please him because he smiled rather contentedly, and said:

'I won't linger too long, *madame*. I am not without discretion, I can assure you.'

'Oh, but—' Ryan licked her lips. 'You'll stay for dinner, won't you?'

The priest shook his head. 'Some wine,' he said, raising his glass, 'and a chance to wish you well, and then I shall be gone.'

Sheer terror stiffened Ryan's legs so that she could scarcely walk across the room. In half an hour – an hour at most – she would be alone with the man who was now her husband. What a fool she had been to imagine she could go through with it!

'Father—' she was beginning desperately, when the door opened behind her and Alain came into the kitchen. He had shed the navy suede suit for green corded pants and a cream sweater, and to her eyes he looked bigger and more powerful than ever. She quaked at the idea of attempting to thwart him. She wouldn't stand a chance, and the law was all on his side now.

As though her pale strained features mirrored her thoughts, Alain's eyes narrowed as they rested upon her. 'Get some glasses, Ryan,' he said harshly. 'I have some champagne on ice for this most special occasion.'

She doubted that the Abbé Maurice was aware of the irony in his tones, but she was aware of it and was glad. Surely, if he could speak so mockingly of the situation, he found no great advantages in it. If only she could believe ...

The Dom Perignon was wasted on her. She had only tasted champagne once before, and it was not something she particularly cared for. She preferred the still, smooth wines to the sparkling ones.

But the Abbé obviously enjoyed toasting them both, and he was warmly expansive as he left.

'May God smile on you, my children,' he declared, taking first Ryan's hand and then Alain's. 'Be thankful for your youth and good health, and may God bless you with many fine sons and daughters to share your good fortune.'

'Thank you, Father.' While Ryan hid her embarrassment, Alain swung open the outer door, allowing a blast of cold air to penetrate the warm kitchen. It was already dusk, and as he reached for his coat he said: 'I'll drive you back, Father. It's too dark for you to see your way clearly, and besides, the track may be slippery.'

The priest protested, but not too strongly, and Alain overruled his polite refusal. 'Very well. Thank you, my boy.' It was strange to hear Alain addressed as a boy. Abbé Maurice raised his arm to Ryan. 'I will not keep him long, little one,' he chuckled, and went out into the night.

Alain didn't look at Ryan as he closed the door, and after the station wagon had driven away down the track she was still standing motionless by the glowing fire.

Then she gathered her wits. If life was to go on as usual, it was up to her not to alter things. It was almost six o'clock. At seven, Alain would expect his evening meal. On the stove was the vegetable stew she had made the previous day. She had planned to serve that with some of the crusty rolls which Marie had brought her from the bakery in the village, following it with fruit and cheese. It was a simple enough meal – most of the meals she prepared were simple meals – but would he expect something more extravagant tonight? After the Dom Perignon she could not be sure.

But nothing had changed, she told herself severely. Just because, for appearances and nothing more, he had produced a bottle of champagne, it did not mean that tonight was some sort of a celebration. A reluctant sob caught in her throat. Her wedding day! Her wedding night! Had any girl had a stranger one?

The table was set, and the stew was simmering on the stove when she heard the station wagon coming back. Immediately her nerves became taut, and a lump closed up her throat. He came in whistling, taking off the leather coat and hanging it behind the door. He went to the sink and washed his hands, drying them on the towel she kept for the purpose, and then sniffed the air appreciatively.

'Mmm, something smells good,' he commented, taking out his cheroots and lighting one from the fire. 'And rolls? Did Marie bring them?'

'Yes.'

Ryan was short, but she couldn't help it. He flicked a glance towards her, and then sighed. 'What is it? What's wrong? Why are you looking so upset? Have I done something wrong?'

Ryan shook her head quickly. 'Of course not.'

'I've told you I had nothing to do with putting your clothes in my bedroom. Don't you believe me?'

Ryan nodded, stirring the stew unnecessarily. 'Sit

46

down. This won't be long.'

There was silence for a long minute, but when she ventured to look round he had not moved. She pressed her lips tightly together and returned her attention to the pan, feeling tension building up inside her. She had started this. It was up to her to finish it. And quickly.

'N – nothing's changed, has it?' she began at last.

His expression hardened. 'Not to my knowledge. Words on a page arouse no motivation in me to behave in any particular manner, no more than their absence would prevent me.'

Ryan looked round at him. 'But until those words were written—' She paused. 'I might have changed my mind.'

He raised his eyes heavenward for a moment, and then inhaled deeply. 'You insist on draining the last ounce of drama out of this situation, do you not? Can you not accept my word, is that it?'

Ryan's hands shook as she twisted them together. 'I – I'm not like you, *monsieur*. I – I find this – all – very strange.'

He put the cheroot between this teeth and regarded her, his hands resting lightly on his hips. 'I am not exactly accustomed to it myself,' he commented dryly. 'And I think perhaps you had better get used to calling me Alain. However, have no fear. I have no intention of invading your bedroom and having my evil way. I realize you find this hard to believe, but I am not attracted by juveniles, little one.'

Ryan flushed scarlet. 'Must you be so offensive!' she exclaimed.

He made an exasperated gesture. 'What is offensive about the truth? I should have thought my words would reassure you.'

Ryan turned back to the stew. 'You're very explicit, *monsieur*. I'll try and remember that.'

'And the name?' He put his head on one side. 'You'll

47

remember that, too? Or do you wish Marie to imagine you call me *monsieur* in bed?'

'Marie?' Ryan faltered.

'Of course. You understand that when you remove your belongings back to your own room she will realize that all is not right between us. Would you have her tell the village that as well as refusing to share my bed you persist in calling me *monsieur*?'

Ryan stared down at her toes. 'Will she? Tell – the village, I mean?'

'It will be a nine days' wonder, nothing more.'

Ryan was not so sure. During the past week she had walked down to the village a couple of times to shop at the bakery and general dealers, and she did not like to think of the speculation which would follow such an announcement, the eyes which would follow her down the street, feeling sympathy for her, perhaps even pitying her. And as for Marie herself . . . Ryan did not like to contemplate her reactions. She would be sure to think that Ryan was a failure.

'Perhaps – perhaps I should leave – leave some of my clothes in – in your room,' she faltered, looking up.

'I think not.' Now Alain was abrupt. He strode across the room to the hall door. 'If you will excuse me . . . I shall be in the study when the meal is ready.'

Later that night, lying sleepless in her own bed, Ryan tried to rationalize her thoughts. What did it matter what Marie thought? What anyone thought? This was no temporary settlement, it was a long term arrangement, and only she and Alain played any part in it. If Marie did notice that all was perhaps not as it should be, she would handle that situation when it arose. After all, she was the mistress of the house, not Marie. Perhaps she had allowed her too much familiarity in the past. She might have to change that in future. The prospect was depressing. Marie was good company, and she had been a good friend in a place where such things were not readily available.

She twisted restlessly between the sheets. She must try to get some sleep and stop tormenting herself with anxieties about the future. Alain would expect her to be up and about as usual in the morning, and it wouldn't do for her to appear with haggard eyes. Or maybe it would. With a slightly hysterical gulp she realized that Marie would expect exactly that.

The sound of a door opening and closing brought her upright in the bed, and she held her breath, listening. But there was no further sound and with a sigh she sank back against the pillows again. But the noise had aroused her, and on impulse she slid out of bed and pulled on her candlewick dressing-gown. Silently she opened her bedroom door and stood in the aperture for a few moments, her ears alert for any sound.

Along the landing, in the pale light of the moon, she could see that Alain's door stood ajar. She guessed he had left his room and gone downstairs, and she walked to the head of the twisting staircase and looked down the well. The hall below was bathed in moonlight, and even as she watched a shadow stalked across the rug-strewn floor. A gasp died in her throat as she realized it was just Tabithe, probably disturbed by the same sound which had disturbed Ryan.

A thread of light could just be discerned beneath the study door, and Ryan drew a trembling breath. So Alain couldn't sleep either. It was reassuring somehow. He was not as insensitive as he would have her believe. She was tempted to go downstairs and offer him a hot drink, but common sense prevented her. Probably the last thing he needed was a hot drink. No doubt something more potent was more in his line.

With a sigh she turned back into her room, closing the door behind her reluctantly. As she shed her dressing-gown and climbed into bed, she reflected with sudden clarity on the years stretching ahead, and wondered why they had never seemed so bleak as they did at this moment.

CHAPTER FOUR

It was a week before Marie made any comment on the fact that Ryan was obviously still sleeping in her old room. They were clearing out the linen cupboard at the time. Ryan had decided she ought to know exactly what linen she possessed just in case they ever had any visitors, although that seemed highly unlikely at the moment.

Marie was counting pillow cases, when she suddenly looked up and said: 'I am sorry things did not work out for you, *madame*.'

Ryan stopped in the middle of folding tablecloths, and stared in embarrassment at the other girl. 'I – I beg your pardon?'

Marie sighed, and put down the pillow cases she was holding. 'I am sorry, *madame*. But I cannot help but notice that – well, that you and Monsieur de Beaunes do not share the same bed.'

Ryan looked down at what she was doing. 'I don't think that's any business of yours, Marie,' she said, in a tight little voice.

Marie continued to regard her sympathetically. 'I know it is not, *madame*. But I have grown fond of you, *madame*, and I do not like to think of you being – unhappy.'

Ryan's facial muscles relaxed somewhat. 'I'm not unhappy, Marie.'

'Not unhappy?' Marie's eyes were wide. 'Oh, *madame*! You do not have to pretend with me.'

'I'm not pretending,' Ryan finished folding the tablecloth in her hands and laid it neatly on the pile with hands which she saw with relief were quite steady. 'Monsieur – Monsieur de Beaunes and I – our marriage is perfectly satisfactory. We – that is – I'm sure you understand

the situation. I always thought marriages of convenience were commonplace here.'

'Marriages – of convenience?' Marie frowned. 'Ah, yes, I understand what you mean. But I do not think you do. Although I admit that in some cases a girl may marry a man who is more suited to her parents than to herself – a marriage of convenience, as you say – it is a *normal* marriage, *madame*. No woman would give herself into a man's care without expecting – oh, you know what I mean.' She paused unhappily. 'In such cases a man may take a mistress, and a woman a lover. But – such physical liberties are in addition to, not instead of a husband, or a wife.'

Ryan's face burned. 'I don't think I want to know about such things, thank you, Marie!' she replied tersely.

Marie looked at her worriedly. 'I am sorry, *madame*,' she said again. 'I – I did not know . . .'

Now it was Ryan's turn to look perplexed. 'What do you mean? What didn't you know?'

Marie shook her head, and began tackling the pillow cases again, muttering to herself, and Ryan felt frustration rising inside her.

'What didn't you know, Marie?' she demanded again.

Marie looked up reluctantly. 'I'd rather not say, *madame*.'

Ryan clenched her fists. 'I'm not – peculiar, if that's what you're thinking!'

'Oh, no, *madame*.' Marie's protest was sincere. 'I did not think you were. Not for one moment. And – well, I have heard that your – that – Monsieur de Beaunes – well, that he is not inexperienced, *madame*.' She was obviously finding this difficult to say. 'I am just sorry you cannot feel the things I feel.'

Ryan's lips moved wordlessly for a moment. 'What things?'

Marie lifted her shoulders in a dismissing way. 'I had

51

heard that the English were cold, *madame*. But I had not believed it.'

Now Ryan understood. 'I see. You think I'm frigid, is that it?'

Marie bent her head. 'I am sorry, *madame*.'

Ryan turned away, unable to stand the look of pitying sympathy on the other girl's face. 'Well, I'm sorry to disappoint you, Marie,' she got out tautly, 'but frigidity doesn't enter into it. My – that is – Monsieur de Beaunes has not – touched me. Nor would I wish him to do so. Our marriage is one of convenience in the truest sense of the word. It was advantageous to both of us to enter into a bond of matrimony, but that is all.'

'Yes, *madame*.'

Patently Marie did not believe her, but there was nothing more Ryan could say to convince her. Already she had said more than she had intended, and she had no doubt that Alain would consider her behaviour less than discreet. But she thrust such thoughts aside. It was hardly likely that he would come to hear what she had been imprudent enough to admit.

The following week there was a letter for Ryan.

Since she had come to France, her only communication had been from her aunt's solicitors in England. The girls she had worked with at the library did not know her address. She had promised to write and give them all the details once she had settled down in France, but her father's death and the subsequent upheaval of her marriage had driven such thoughts from her head. Besides, she would have found it very hard to explain the reasons for her precipitate marriage to them.

So it was surprising that she should receive any mail at all, particularly a letter with a French postmark. Marie brought it when she arrived for work that morning, and as Alain had already left for the plant, Ryan took the letter into the study to read in private.

The address in Paris was unfamiliar, and so too was the

signature at the end – Louise Ferrier. But the surname had been her father's and she assumed the woman must be some relation of his.

She was right. Louise Ferrier had been the wife of Emile Ferrier, her grandfather's brother. She had just heard of her nephew's death, and his daughter's marriage to Alain de Beaunes. She had always wanted to meet her nephew's child, she said, and she invited her to come to Paris, with her husband, and spend a few days with a lonely old woman. Now that her husband was dead she had no one, and she would love to see them both.

Ryan read the letter twice before putting it back into the envelope. It was strangely warming to feel that somewhere there was someone who cared about her. She got up and walked across to the window. Last night the wind had blown traces of snow down from the mountains, and rain had lashed the windows. It would be Christmas soon, a time for reuniting families.

When Alain arrived home at lunchtime, she presented him with the letter, and he turned it over inquiringly.

'What is this?'

'Read it.' Ryan seated herself across the table from him, excitement heightening the colour in her cheeks. 'It's from my father's aunt.'

Alain considered the writing on the envelope without opening it. 'Louise Ferrier?' he asked, his mouth twisting slightly.

'Yes, that's right. Why? Have you met her? Do you know her?'

'I know of her,' he amended, putting the letter down on the table. 'Mmm, this smells good. What is it?'

Ryan gave an exasperated exclamation. 'It's *bouilla-baisse*. Don't you recognize it?' She tasted the fish soup experimentally. '*Oh!*' It had a slightly burned taste. She picked up a roll and tore it in half. 'Aren't you going to read the letter?'

'It's addressed to you.'

Ryan sighed. 'That doesn't matter. You're – you're my husband!' She flushed.

'Yes, I am.' He spooned soup into his mouth, applying himself to the meal.

Ryan shifted uncomfortably. 'Please read it. She says she's just heard about – about my father's death. She – she's invited us to visit her – in Paris.'

Alain said nothing. He continued to drink his soup, occasionally pausing to swallow some of the wine he had poured into his glass. Ryan watched him, toying with her own food, unable to understand his lack of interest. At last, she said: 'Well? Haven't you anything to say?'

Alain looked up, and she noticed inconsequently how long were the dark lashes which fringed his tawny eyes. The heavy lids half shaded their surveillance, as he said: 'What do you expect me to say?'

Ryan made a helpless gesture. 'I don't know. Whether we can go to Paris, I suppose.'

'Do you want to go to Paris?'

Ryan couldn't sustain the penetration of those dark pupils. She looked down at her plate. 'Well, it will be Christmas in three weeks. I thought it might be nice . . .'

Alain shook his head, pouring more wine into his glass. 'All right. Go, if you want to.'

Ryan's head jerked up then. 'You mean – on my own?'

'Well, I shan't be going,' he returned flatly.

Ryan felt the little bubble of excitement inside her burst and evaporate. 'But I can't go on my own,' she protested.

'Why not?' He raised his glass to his lips and surveyed her over the rim.

Ryan plucked at her roll, shedding crumbs all over the table. 'I – I just can't, that's all. Besides, Paris is a long way away. It would mean staying overnight at least.'

Alain's eyes hardened. 'Stay as long as you like. I'm perfectly capable of staying here on my own.'

'No!' The word was torn from her, and he looked at her strangely.

'Why so vehement?'

Ryan hunched her shoulders, resting her elbows on the table. 'It – it will be our – our first Christmas together,' she mumbled, into her hand.

Alain thrust back his chair and got to his feet then, looking down at her bleakly. 'I hope you are not becoming sentimental, Ryan,' he said harshly. 'There will be many more Christmases to spend together, each one no different from the last!' And with these grim words he left her.

After the door had closed behind him, Ryan drank no more of her soup but gathered the dirty dishes together and put them into the sink. She hesitated over the wine in her glass, but then swallowed it carelessly. Why was it, she thought resentfully, that every time she tried to behave normally, he felt the need to set her down? She thought she had done quite well in the circumstances, coping with the housework and the shopping, asking little of him but civility. The terrifying realities of a sexual relationship being thrust upon her had receded, and in fact he seldom referred to their association. Occasionally when he told her he was going out in the evening, after dinner, she wondered about that side of his nature, but her own fears had been replaced by a grudging respect.

Sometimes she wished he would talk to her more, for it was a lonely existence she was living, but always he seemed to find other things to do. She would have liked to have talked to him about her father, and about his private life before he came to Bellaise. She knew so little about him – whether he had any relatives, who had been his first wife, and how had she died, whether in fact there had been any children from that union. She didn't think there could have been. Little as she knew about him, she sensed he would not shirk that kind of responsibility. But, as he discouraged any attempt on her part to put their relationship on a more companionable footing, she doubted she would ever know. He was polite to her, punctual for meals, he appreciated what she did about the house; but he gave her no more attention than he would a house-keeper, and a faint resentment was stirring inside her. No matter that her father had been the instigator of this situ-ation, Alain had practically forced her into accepting it; surely it was up to him to try and make it as pleasant as possible for her.

During the next few days the letter was constantly on Ryan's mind. Alain did not mention it again; apparently, so far as he was concerned, the matter was closed, but Ryan was far from satisfied. She didn't really know what to do. She was tempted to reply to Louise Ferrier that although her husband was too busy to make the trip to Paris, she would come herself, but she put off making such a big decision. Besides, for some reason which she didn't altogether understand, she was loath to go away and leave him alone for several days. She had no doubt that he would be capable of taking care of himself, and Marie was always around to cope with the housework, but something held her back. So long as she was here, she could pretend that things were normal, even though she knew they were not, but if she went to Paris and had to tell this woman a lot of lies, how would things seem on her return? The human brain was an odd creation. It saw what it wanted to see and no further. Was her existence here so unacceptable that she was afraid to view it with the objectivity distance might give? she asked herself. But she knew it wasn't entirely that either, and as there were other daily problems to contend with, she postponed her reply.

One morning, about a week before Christmas, Alain told her he was going into Anciens, and asked whether she would like to accompany him. Ryan was taken aback by his unexpected invitation, and as she had been rather cool towards him lately she wondered whether this was in the nature of an apology.

'I suppose I could come and buy a few things for Christmas,' she murmured thoughtfully. Since their marriage, Alain made her an allowance from the estate as well as paying all the housekeeping bills in the village.

Alain shrugged, regarding her with vague impatience. 'Well, if you do want to come, you'd better hurry. I want to leave in half an hour.'

Ryan looked at him indignantly. 'But I haven't made the beds yet – and there's the dishes—'

'Marie is coming, is she not?'

'I suppose so.'

'Then she can do the dishes and make the beds. Her work here is not arduous, you see to that.'

Ryan sensed a hidden meaning to his words, but she hadn't the time to question them. Instead, she put their breakfast dishes into the sink, and then ran upstairs to change.

For the first time she felt like making the most of herself, and she hastily pulled a cream-skirted suit from her wardrobe, and put this on together with a royal blue shirt. Knee-length suede boots encased her slender legs, and a hooded suede coat, edged with shaggy cream fur, completed the ensemble. She knew she looked good, the thick chestnut hair emerging in curling tendrils against her cheeks, and her spirits rose.

If Alain was impressed by her appearance, he managed not to show it, and she felt a ridiculous sense of disappointment which she quickly squashed. What was the matter with her? she asked herself angrily. She didn't care what he thought of her. Her reasons for getting dressed up stemmed from the knowledge that she was going to town where there would be other eyes to appraise her and admire her.

Alain had not bothered to change, but the fur-lined leather coat and dark trousers suited his sombre countenance. To her annoyance, Ryan found her eyes drawn to him in the car, and she decided, rather maliciously, that it was that brooding masculinity which she disliked most about him. His thick hair needed cutting and strayed over his collar at the back, and the sideburns which grew down his cheeks showed the toughness of the beard he shaved from his jaw. But his hair always bore the sheen of good health, she had to admit, and although he used no hair dressing it lay thick and smooth against his head. He smelt of shaving lotion and tobacco, and something else – something which she decided was the clean male smell of his body. Turning her attention to the mountainous slopes ahead of them, she supposed she ought to consider herself fortunate that he bathed every day. Not all men were so particular about personal hygiene. He could have been like Henri Vachelle, who worked for the Abbé Maurice, attending to the cleaning of the church and keeping the yard tidy. He was just a young man, in his late twenties, Ryan guessed, and he always watched her closely whenever she passed him, revealing in the caressing darkness of his eyes that he was attracted to her. But he smelled of sweat and stale wine, and his fingernails were dirty. Ryan had always thought that she could never allow any man to touch her who had dirty fingernails. Alain's fingers were long and brown, but the nails were square cut and clean. She wondered how it would feel to have a man's hands probing the secret places of her body, and felt a wave of heat sweep over her. She brought herself up short, controlling her quickened breathing, but just for a moment the images in her mind had given way to Alain de Beaunes' dark face.

Alain flicked back his cuff at that moment and consulted the plain gold watch on his wrist. 'I have some business to attend to when we reach Anciens,' he said, without looking at her. 'I suggest you spend the time doing whatever shopping you intend to do, and then we can meet and have lunch before coming back.'

Ryan was still shocked by the duplicity of her own

body, and her reply was short and offhand. 'If you like.'

He looked at her then, his eyes narrowed and interrogative. 'Is something wrong? Do you not wish to meet me for lunch?'

'Oh – yes. Of course.' Ryan ran a nervous hand over her hair.

He shrugged. 'It was a suggestion, nothing more. If there is something you would rather do . . .'

'There's not,' she broke in on him. 'Have you no shopping that you want to do?'

He shook his head. 'Anything I need is catered for quite adequately at Bellaise,' he replied.

'I can believe it.' Ryan was bitter.

'And what is that supposed to mean?'

She coloured. 'Nothing. I – I was just agreeing with you.'

His fingers tightened round the wheel and she saw the whitening of his knuckles. She tore her eyes away, and stared tensely down at her own hands. *I hate him*, she told herself fiercely, but she knew that he was not to blame for her sudden awareness of him.

There was silence for a few minutes, and then he said quietly: 'If your behaviour is due to frustration over Louise Ferrier's invitation, then I suggest you make arrangements to spend several days in Paris. The shops there are bound to be more exciting than those in Anciens.'

Ryan's head jerked up and she stared at him resentfully. 'I don't know what you mean.'

'Yes, you do. For days now you've been sulking, and haven't had a word to say for yourself. Now that you've found your tongue, it's unnecessarily sharp.'

'I didn't think you noticed,' she retorted scornfully, and had the satisfaction of seeing his facial muscles grow taut.

'I noticed,' he returned, in a controlled voice. 'You're not very adept at hiding your feelings.'

'But you are, I suppose.'

'I'm considerably more adept than you are,' he agreed, with infuriating calmness. 'Otherwise I might well have said something I'd have later regretted after learning that you'd been discussing our personal affairs with all and sundry!'

Now Ryan was taken aback. 'Discussing our affairs with all and sundry?' she echoed blankly. 'I – I don't know what you're talking about.'

'Don't you? But you have discussed our – relationship with Marie, haven't you?'

Ryan moved restlessly. 'I – I may have said something.'

'More than that. You virtually told her that you wouldn't let me touch you!'

'I – I didn't!'

'She feels sorry for you, of course, but she feels equally sorry for me. I warned you what she was like. She feels I need – well, consolation.'

Ryan gasped. This was terrible. Hiding her dismay in anger, she demanded: 'And how did you get to know what I had said?'

'That's my business.'

'Oh, is it?' Ryan half turned in her seat towards him. 'Perhaps Marie told you herself. Perhaps you – console yourself with her. Perhaps that's why you're so keen for me to go to Paris!'

As soon as the words were uttered, Ryan wished she could retract them. They sounded so silly, so childish; impossibly jealous. What on earth had possessed her to say such things to him!

Alain looked sideways at her, and there was a hint of humour in the sardonic twist of his mouth. 'I think you're getting into very deep water, little one,' he commented lazily. 'But if it's of any interest to you, Marie is not my type.'

Thereafter there was silence until they reached Anciens.

Anciens stood at the confluence of the Bajou and the Rhone. This was lush pastoral land, which in summer would graze the fat white Charollais cattle. The embankment was lined with poplars, and narrow streets led to the market square where one could buy practically anything. There were stalls selling meat, and fish, tiny sardines from the south and lobsters from Brittany, hams and cheeses of every kind. There was the smell of freshly baked bread, and pastries filled with cream and nuts to melt the most rigid diet. Tall houses, some with balconies still boasted window boxes bright with geraniums and thickly petalled roses, that defied the winds that whistled down the valley as the snows fell on the Alps.

Ryan was enchanted. She forgot her antagonism towards Alain and exclaimed at the rich variety of it all. Alain answered her questions goodnaturedly, and parked the station wagon in a small mews off the market square.

As Ryan would have scrambled out, he stopped her, his fingers hard about the flesh of her forearm. 'One moment. Do you need any money?'

Ryan flushed. 'No. You give me a generous allowance.'

Alain continued to consider her heated face. 'Nevertheless, at this time of year there are bound to be extra expenses.' He released her to take his wallet from his inside pocket. 'Here!' He held out a handful of notes. 'Buy yourself something pretty for Christmas.'

Ryan shook her head, not taking the money, and he uttered an imprecation. 'Take it! It's a gift. Buy yourself a present from me.'

'I'd rather not,' she retorted proudly. Wives did not buy their own gifts. Their husbands surprised them with something special. Only she was no ordinary wife, and he was no ordinary husband.

'Why not?' He flicked quickly through the notes. 'Isn't it enough?'

Ryan gasped. 'Oh, how can you ask such a thing! I don't want your money. I have money of my own.'

Alain's expression changed, showing comprehension. 'Ah! Do you expect me to produce a present on Christmas morning, is that it?' he inquired, half derisively.

'I don't expect anything of you!' she declared, and thrust open her door and got out before he could stop her.

The cold air hit her after the warmth of the car, and she quickly drew up the hood of her coat. She was tucking strands of hair inside when he got out and walked round the car to join her.

'Will you be all right?' he queried, looking down at her with unexpectedly gentle eyes.

Ryan felt a curious weakness in her stomach and the stupid prick of tears behind her eyes. 'I should think so,' she replied, her voice unnecessarily abrupt in her efforts to hide the effect he was having on her. Perhaps it was as well that he usually treated her with such detachment. She was finding it extremely difficult to remain immune from the not inconsiderable charm he was choosing to exert.

He glanced again at his watch. 'It is half past ten. I suggest we meet for lunch in say – two hours? Will that be long enough for you?'

Ryan nodded, biting her lips. 'But I don't know my way about. You'll have to direct me.'

He took her upper arm between his fingers, and escorted her along a cobbled street to the market square. Then he drew her attention to a group of municipal buildings facing them. 'I shall be there for most of the morning,' he told her. 'If you need me, don't hesitate to come in. Otherwise I suggest we meet at Le Dauphin at half past twelve.' He pointed to the small hotel with its striped awnings and white painted shutters.

Ryan was overwhelmingly conscious of his fingers gripping her arm and of the closeness of his hard male body.

She had the most ridiculous desire to hold on to him and tell him that she didn't want to leave him and go shopping alone. It was more than two months since she had visited a town, and she told herself it was the busy thoroughfare and the crowds of unfamiliar faces which aroused such a feeling of panic at his proposed departure. But the almost possessive need she had to stay with him was not entirely due to her surroundings. She really did want to stay with him, and her interest in the shops had dwindled accordingly.

'Well?' He was looking down at her, waiting for her answer, and she tried to gather her wits. But when she looked up at him, a little of what she was feeling must have shown in her eyes, because his eyes darkened perceptibly, and his brows drew together in a frown. 'What is it?' he demanded huskily. 'Why are you looking at me like that?' His fingers encircled her arm. 'Ryan, for God's sake, what did I say?'

One of her hands probed the fastening of his coat as though she would hold him away from her, but her voice was unsteady as she said: 'I – I – Alain, I—'

'Now why is it that one always meets one's friends in the market place at Anciens?'

The light feminine voice destroyed the moment of intimacy between them, and Ryan turned frustratedly to face the woman who was standing behind her. She was a tall woman, in her late twenties or early thirties, Ryan guessed, with a generously proportioned body which was sinuously accentuated by close-fitting nylon slacks and a chunky scarlet sweater. Her hair was blonde and curly and framed a face which even Ryan had to admit was very attractive.

Alain had released Ryan at the appearance of the newcomer, and now he smiled. 'Hello, Vivienne,' he greeted her, with obvious pleasure. 'I didn't know you were coming to Anciens today.'

'Nor I you,' she countered, her blue eyes flickering calculatingly over Ryan. 'I'd have begged a lift. As it is I've brought the car.'

Alain glanced thoughtfully at his wife, and then said: 'Ryan, this is Madame Couvrier, a neighbour of ours at Bellaise.'

'How do you do?' Ryan was polite, but her brain was working furiously. Alain and this woman obviously knew one another very well, and the confidence with which Vivienne Couvrier talked about begging a lift revealed an intimacy which Ryan found unpleasant to contemplate.

'So you're Alain's wife!' Vivienne was speaking to her now, and Ryan did not mistake the mockery in her tones. 'You're very young, aren't you?' The words implied a rebuke for which Ryan had no answer.

Alain intervened. 'Are you in Anciens on business, Vivienne, or is it a shopping trip?'

'Mostly shopping, *chéri*. And you?'

'I have some business to attend to,' he admitted, glancing at Ryan. 'My – wife – has some shopping to do.'

Vivienne's eyes narrowed speculatively. 'Has she? Then perhaps we should join forces. It would enable us to get to know one another. You've kept her to yourself long enough, Alain.'

There was more mockery now, and Ryan turned dismayed eyes up to her husband. The last thing she wanted was to have to spend the morning in the company of a woman who would clearly derive a great deal of enjoyment from making fun of her. But Alain chose to ignore her silent plea.

'That's not a bad idea, actually, Vivienne. Ryan is a stranger here, and I was a bit doubtful about leaving her alone. She speaks quite good French, but the dialects here might confuse her. Would you mind?'

'Oh, really, Alain, I'll be all right—' Ryan began desperately, but Vivienne was nodding her head.

'Your husband knows best, *chérie*. We can have a

64

gossip over coffee later, and at lunch?' She looked expectantly at Alain.

'We were meeting for lunch at Le Dauphin. Would you care to join us?'

'I would love to.'

Vivienne was highly satisfied now, but Ryan was furiously angry. How dared Alain arrange her morning for her with a complete disregard for her feelings. Just because earlier he had imagined something was troubling her, did not give him the right to put her into the hands of this woman like a fractious child.

But there was nothing she could do. Short of making a scene and refusing outright to go with Vivienne Couvrier, she had to accept their arrangements, and Alain gave her a curt little smile before striding away across the square.

With his departure, Vivienne lost her air of vivacity. 'What do you want to buy?' she asked in rather bored tones, and Ryan thrust her hands into her pockets.

'I don't know yet,' she replied honestly.

Vivienne heaved an exaggerated sigh. 'Oh! You're not one of those window-shoppers, are you?'

'Yes.' Ryan derived an immense amount of pleasure out of seeing Vivienne's irritation. 'But you don't have to accompany me, you know. You can meet me a few minutes before we have to meet Alain, if you like.'

Vivienne's eyes narrowed. 'I think not, *chérie*,' she declined dryly. 'Oh, come on. We're blocking the footpath. Let's go along here. There are several department stores, and a new boutique called La Roue.' She considered Ryan's slender figure. 'They cater for teenagers, I believe.'

Ryan let the barbed comment ride. She had the sense to realize that in any argument with Vivienne Couvrier, she was likely to emerge the loser. The older girl had age and experience on her side, and she had obviously not been brought up with Ryan's inhibitions about being polite whatever the provocation.

And to some extent, as the morning progressed, Ryan's anger abated. Vivienne knew the town well, and guessed instinctively which stores would interest her young charge. Once inside, much to her relief, Ryan was left to her own devices while Vivienne wandered off to talk to the salesgirls, many of whom, she explained, came from the village.

Ryan bought several things – cosmetics and perfume, personal toiletries, tights, even some after shaving lotion for Alain, which she told herself was to keep just in case he had bought anything for her. Her most expensive purchases were a cream cashmere sweater and a brown velvet caftan, embroidered with multi-coloured threads of silk at the wide cuffs and hem. Its soft folds hinted at the slender curves beneath, and she wondered, rather apprehensively, what Alain would think of it.

Her worst moment came in the small bistro where Vivienne decided they would have coffee. The bistro was full and crowded with shoppers, but somehow Vivienne managed to find an empty space in a corner. They had coffee and pastries, Ryan with her lap overflowing with bags, and watched the hectic scene outside the windows. A vendor was auctioning some geese, and the sound of their squawking filled the air. White feathers flew by the window and Ryan found herself remembering last Christmas in England with Aunt Maggie. It was not the first time she had thought about her aunt, but briefly she felt a wave of homesickness sweep over her. And yet for what? She had no home in England any longer.

Vivienne's words, when they came, were doubly disturbing because of her sudden vulnerability. 'I know why Alain married you, you know.'

Dragging her thoughts back to the present, Ryan blinked at her companion. 'Do you?'

'Yes. Alain told me, of course.'

Ryan wondered why 'of course', but she didn't question

66

it. 'I see.'

'And how long do you expect it to last?' Vivienne went on, almost as though she was discussing the weather. She was completely oblivious of eavesdroppers, although Ryan supposed in the crowded café no one would overhear what she was saying.

'How – long?' She tried to sound composed. 'I don't think I understand, *madame*.'

'You must. You're female, aren't you, even if you are hardly a woman! It's a most unsatisfactory state of affairs. You know that sooner or later it will have to be annulled.'

'Annulled?' Ryan wished she could stop repeating everything Vivienne said, but her brain refused to function. 'I – I don't think it's any of your business, *madame*.'

Vivienne glanced round, and then leant towards her confidingly. 'I – er – I'm very fond of Alain, my dear. I've known him for more than nine years – ever since he came to Bellaise, in fact. Naturally, I care about his happiness.'

Ryan juggled with the parcels on her lap and managed to get her coffee to her lips. 'I appreciate your concern, *madame*,' she said stiffly, 'but I don't think I should discuss such things with you. I'm sure you would object were I to question you about your marriage.'

'I'm a widow, *chérie*,' replied Vivienne airily. 'Gilles, my husband, died three years ago. He was considerably older than me, and developed a heart complaint within a year of our marriage.' She paused. 'You see, I know about these things. I married Gilles because he was a wealthy widower with a thriving business. Oh, our positions were not identical. Alain is only twenty years older than you, whereas Gilles was almost forty years older than me. But there are similarities. Gilles was already in his sixties, with a grown family, whereas I was a mere girl of twenty-three. Everyone knew the situation. Gilles got someone to share his last few years, and I became the owner of the

Couvrier garage.'

Ryan was appalled at the callousness Vivienne displayed. She was not used to such plain speaking, particularly not about things which she had always regarded as private and personal. And she also knew, with an insight she had not previously possessed, that had Alain been a man in his sixties, she could not have married him whatever her father's wishes might have been. It was a startling revelation. Why should it matter to her how old Alain was? If their marriage was to remain one of convenience, his age should not come into it. But it did.

She looked nervously at the clock on the wall of the bistro. 'It's after twelve,' she pointed out, with some relief. 'Oughtn't we to be making our way back to the hotel in the square? Alain said he would meet us there at twelve-thirty, didn't he?'

Vivienne lighted a long cigarette, ignoring Ryan's suggestion. 'Tell me,' she said, inhaling deeply and allowing the smoke to drift out through her nostrils. 'Tell me – don't you find life at Bellaise a little dull? I mean, after your life in England? A girl of your age – and appearance – must have had lots of boy-friends, lots of outings to look forward to.'

Ryan resigned herself to another few minutes. 'No, *madame*,' she replied. 'I don't find Bellaise at all dull. I never was particularly keen on going out a lot. I lived with my aunt, and although she didn't discourage me from having friends, I was quite content to spend my time with her. I read a lot, and I used to watch television—'

'Yes, yes.' Vivienne was plainly not interested in her activities except in so far as they reflected upon her life in France. 'But you must have had some boy-friends, *chérie.*'

Ryan sighed. 'One or two. They bored me mostly. They were only interested in girls and pop music and making money – not necessarily in that order.'

Vivienne tapped ash into the overflowing tray with obvious impatience. 'You came to France when your aunt died, I believe.'

'That's right. Four days before my father died too.'

Vivienne's lips twisted. 'Yes. That was most unfortunate.'

But Ryan had the feeling she was meaning unfortunate for herself, rather than for Pierre Ferrier.

'I think we really ought to be going,' she said again. 'The town is so busy. We should give ourselves plenty of time—'

'Oh, very well.' Vivienne squashed out the half-smoked cigarette with ill-concealed impatience. 'Alain *will* wait, *chérie*. I can assure you of that.'

When they reached the hotel there was no sign of Alain, but at Vivienne's insistence they went inside and found him seated on a stool by the bar, drinking something long and cool. He got to his feet when he saw them, and glanced pointedly at his watch.

'I know, I know, we're late,' exclaimed Vivienne, before Ryan could say anything. 'But this child insisted on buying up the whole store! Look at her – loaded down with parcels! I don't know what on earth she's been buying.'

Alain came towards them and divested Ryan of her larger packages. 'We should have arranged to meet at the car,' he remarked. 'Then we could have got rid of these.'

'It's all right. I can manage,' replied Ryan, still stung by Vivienne's deliberate attempt to discredit her, but Alain ignored her protests and a word with the receptionist had the parcels piled safely behind her desk to be retrieved on their departure.

'Now—' he said, leading Ryan back into the bar. 'What will you drink?'

Ryan didn't enjoy lunch, but then she hadn't expected to do so. Vivienne dominated the conversation, talking mainly with Alain, and in that intimate confidential manner which excluded all outsiders. Ryan had to concede that Alain did his best from time to time to draw her into the conversation, but as she mostly answered in monosyllables anything that was said to her, it discouraged his efforts.

At last the meal was over, and it was time for them to leave. Vivienne rose to her feet with evident reluctance, her cheeks flushed from the amount of wine she had consumed. Ryan thought the cognac she had had with her coffee must have made her reckless, because her fingers curled round Alain's arm, and looking up at him provocatively, she said: 'Will I see you later, *chéri*?'

Ryan turned away, putting on her coat with nobody's assistance, going towards the receptionist's desk to collect her belongings. But Alain released himself from Vivienne and forestalled her, collecting the packages himself and preventing Ryan's attempts to take them from him with a cold hard stare.

Outside, the air was cooling perceptibly as the afternoon wore on. Vivienne shivered and looked irritably at Alain. '*Au revoir, chéri*,' she murmured. '*Au revoir*, Ryan. You must come and have tea with me one afternoon. That is what the English like to do, is it not? We could – talk over – experiences.'

Ryan forced a smile. 'Thank you, *madame*.'

Vivienne shrugged and looked again at Alain. 'So – I will go.'

Alain nodded. '*Au revoir*, Vivienne. Drive carefully.'

'You, too.'

Vivienne left them, walking away across the square, her hips swinging, and Ryan deliberately glanced round. 'Where's the car?' she asked, in a cold little voice.

'This way.'

Alain went ahead, threading his way between the lingering groups of shoppers that thronged those stalls which had not already packed up. The mews where they had left the station wagon was tightly packed with cars, and for a moment Ryan thought they would not be able to get out. Alain opened the car and tossed her packages carelessly on to the back seat before swinging the door wider for her to get in. She was tempted to tell him that there were breakable articles amongst the parcels he had thrown in so carelessly, but his face deterred any protest. He slammed her door shut behind her and then walked round the bonnet to get in beside her, his leg brushing hers as he adjusted his clothes for comfort.

It soon became apparent that he had parked the vehicle in such a way that he could not have been blocked by other cars, and with effortless expertise he negotiated the narrow passageway between two vehicles and emerged at the entrance to the mews. Ryan breathed a sigh of relief as the narrow streets which led to the market square were left behind for the wider thoroughfare of the embankment. Lights had been lit along the river, strips of coloured bulbs strung from trees, that gave the place a fairylike appearance.

Alain made no comment on the decorations, but his silence had given Ryan time to regret her earlier annoyance. The unpleasantness in the hotel had been magnified by the morning she had spent in Vivienne's company, and although he had been responsible for that, too, she began to appreciate the dilemma Vivienne had placed him in. After all, it had not been so bad. She had bought some delightful things, and that was what she had come for, wasn't it?

With this in mind, therefore, she made a determined effort to behave as though nothing untoward had happened. 'Did you manage to do what you came to do?' she inquired politely.

There was silence for so long that she almost began to believe that he had not heard her. But then, in harsh tones which shook her assumed composure, he demanded: 'Did you have to make your dislike of Madame

Couvrier so apparent?'

Ryan's momentary softening towards him was shattered. His words shocked her into instinctive defence. 'I beg your pardon?'

'Your behaviour towards Vivienne Couvrier.' Alain shook his head. 'Must you constantly demonstrate your lack of maturity by acting like a petulant brat?'

Ryan gasped. 'How – how dare you?'

'I dare because it's the truth. Gilles Couvrier was a friend of your father's. Do you not have the decency to behave politely to his widow?'

'Who is a friend of yours, I suppose?' Ryan countered spitefully.

Alain's lips tightened. 'Vivienne is a friend, yes.'

'A very close friend, I should imagine.' Ryan stared mutinously through the windows, aware that she was trembling.

'Why do you say that?'

Ryan made a helpless gesture. She had spoken impulsively the words which had sprung to her lips, but now she had to clarify her statement and she didn't know how. 'I'd rather not talk about it,' she declared tremulously.

'Is that why you treated us to that display of childish ill manners?' he asked, coldly, flicking a glance in her direction. 'Because you were no longer the centre of attraction?'

Ryan gasped. 'Of course not.' She tugged at the fur on her cuffs. 'Why should I care how you conduct yourself with other women?'

'You have no idea how I conduct myself with other women!' he retorted.

'Perhaps it's just as well.'

'Why? Ours is not a normal marriage. You cannot both have your cake and eat it. Is not that what they say in your country?'

'I am half French,' she reminded him.

'Nevertheless, you still think as an English girl thinks. I

72

think you would like to direct my actions, control my behaviour as an English wife would.'

Ryan stared at him furiously. 'Oh, do you? Well, you're very much mistaken. I don't care what you and Vivienne Couvrier do together!'

But she did! No matter how she might deny it, she was beginning to feel a certain amount of possessiveness towards Alain, and although this was motivated as much by selfishness as anything, it still troubled her.

'I think you have behaved rather foolishly,' he concluded. 'I can only hope that Vivienne did not notice your feline irritability was directed towards her. I assume a certain amount of ill humour was aroused by her innocent explanation of the reasons you were late for lunch. I can assure you, I didn't object—'

Ryan couldn't let that go. 'It wasn't my fault that we were late!' she declared hotly.

'Wasn't it?' He spoke in the resigned tone of a parent.

'No, it wasn't. If you must know, your precious Madame Couvrier took me into a bistro and proceeded to subject me to a third degree!'

'A third degree?' He frowned, obviously perplexed.

'Oh, you know! An inquisition – questions.' She sighed. 'As a matter of fact she asked me how long our marriage was expected to last.'

She delivered this statement with a certain amount of satisfaction, and then felt abominably spiteful as his brows drew together even closer. 'She asked you how long our marriage was expected to last?' he repeated. 'And what did you answer?'

Ryan flushed. 'I don't think I did.' She linked her fingers together. 'She asked me lots of things. I didn't say much at all.'

Alain shook his head. 'Women! How can any mere male hope to understand them?'

Ryan looked at him out of the corners of her eyes. She

73

wondered what he would say if she told him Vivienne had also implied the relationship between them which she had later endeavoured to demonstrate. She had the feeling that while he might choose to live his life to his own satisfaction, he would not care for the woman of his choice to spread their affair too widely.

Ryan turned in her lips and pressed them together. Why was it that this information was so hard for her to accept? She had known for some time that somewhere there must be a woman with whom he could share a physical relationship. But until now it had seemed nebulous, insubstantial. There had been no face to put against his on a white pillow, no body beneath the strength of his powerful thighs. But suddenly there was a face, and a provocative, voluptuous body, and the dream had become harsh reality. How harsh she would never have believed possible.

'I would suggest,' he said at length, when the silence between them had become charged and strained. 'I would suggest that you tell anyone who has recourse to question you to address their inquiries to me in future. And I'm sorry if Vivienne upset you by her tactlessness.'

The unexpectedness of his apology was an upsetting influence after the tension of the last few minutes and Ryan felt the foolish tears pricking her eyes again. When she did not reply to his suggestion, Alain glanced at her once more.

'Now what is wrong?'

'Nothing.' Ryan brushed a hand carelessly across her eyes.

'I cannot agree.' He sighed. 'There are bound to be teething pains in this marriage of ours, Ryan. There are bound to be occasions when you find it impossible to feel any sense of optimism towards the future. But what you have to understand is that everyone feels this way from time to time. Even the most successful marriages have their unsteady beginnings.'

74

'Yes. But ours isn't a – marriage, is it?' she muttered.

'What are you trying to say?' His voice hardened. 'Do you wish it were?'

'No.' Ryan's cheeks flamed. 'No, of course not.' She made a nervous gesture. 'I just meant that – that our – our relationship is bound to be – more difficult than most, isn't it?'

'I see.' Alain's mouth turned down at the corners. 'Tell me – was there something more Vivienne said? Something you have not told me?'

'What could there be?' Ryan moved her shoulders defensively.

He frowned deeply. 'I do not know.' He stared out at the darkening skies. 'There was a time ...' His voice trailed away. 'It is not important. Now, did you enjoy spending your money?'

Ryan tried to summon up enthusiasm to tell him what she had bought, but it would not come. She related her purchases like a child saying its catechism withholding only the knowledge of the brown velvet caftan. Some foolish whim made her wish for him to see her wearing it without that foreknowledge, although in the circumstances it was totally illogical.

CHAPTER FIVE

With Marie's help, Ryan determinedly made some paper streamers and decorated the kitchen and the front parlour. She didn't really know whether there was any likelihood of either Alain or herself using the parlour over the festive season, but it seemed the only logical choice. It was still a cold and austere room, and even with a fire blazing in the hearth had little to commend it. She wondered whether after Christmas she might persuade Alain to have the place redecorated, with perhaps a couple of comfortable chairs instead of the stiff-backed ones that presently occupied either side of the fireplace.

Then, two days before Christmas, Marie had some interesting news for her.

'An Englishman is coming,' she announced, as she took off her coat and hung it on the peg in the kitchen that morning. 'An Englishman is coming to the school, *madame*. To teach the children, you understand. Is not that exciting? Someone from your own country?'

Ryan was intrigued, but she said rather briskly: 'You forget, Marie, I am just as French as I am English.'

Marie smiled. 'Ah, yes, *madame*. But you still speak our language as the English speak it, and you know you will enjoy speaking in English again.'

Ryan uttered an exclamation. 'What do you mean? *I* will enjoy speaking in English again? I may never meet the man.'

'Oh, *madame*, you must. It is the natural thing for you to invite him to dine. That you, as someone who has recently left his country, should welcome him to Bellaise.'

Ryan felt a shiver of anticipation. 'I don't know,' she murmured doubtfully. 'We'll have to see.'

'Yes, *madame*,' Marie seemed well pleased. 'Yes, *madame*, we will see.'

When Ryan mentioned the advent of the Englishman to Alain over their evening meal, however, he seemed less than enthusiastic.

'We have had English tutors at the school before,' he commented off-puttingly. 'They don't stay long. The village is too quiet for them. They soon accept a position in Lyon or Paris. I am sorry if I disappoint you, little one, but I doubt you will find that this man is any different.'

'You don't disappoint me at all,' retorted Ryan, stung by the derisiveness of his tone. 'I told Marie that there was every likelihood I wouldn't even get to meet the man.'

Alain toyed with the spongy dessert she had placed before him. 'What did Marie say? Did she suggest you should do so.'

Ryan couldn't control the colour that filled her cheeks. 'I – she said something like that. I – er – I suppose she thinks I'm lonely.'

'And are you?' His eyes were suddenly intent.

She looked down at her own plate. 'Sometimes,' she answered honestly.

'I see.' He sounded irritated.

'Well! You never talk to me!' she flared, looking up at him. 'Except about the weather – or the state of my health. Oh, and just occasionally about the vines.'

'And what would you have me talk about?'

She shrugged uncomfortably. 'I don't know. Lots of things. You never talk about yourself. About what you did – where you lived – before you came here.'

'Ah, I see.' He swallowed a mouthful of his dessert. 'It is my past which arouses your curiosity.'

'Why not? You know practically everything there is to know about me, while I know next to nothing about you!'

He pushed his plate aside and lifted his wine glass. 'It was all a long time ago. It would not interest you.'

'It would!' She sighed frustratedly as the familiar mask of withdrawal covered his face. 'After all, I should at least know your first wife's name.'

He raised dark eyebrows. 'Very well. Her name was Julia. Julia Marron, before she married me. Does that satisfy you?'

Of course it did not, but Ryan could hardly say so. 'You – you must have been very young when you married her,' she ventured.

He reached for his cheroots. 'I was old enough.' He made as if to get up to light a spill from the fire, but she forestalled him, lighting a spill herself and holding the flaming end to his cheroot. She was familiar enough with his ways now to know that had he risen he would have excused himself and she would have had to serve his coffee in the study, leaving her alone again.

He thanked her, sitting looking at her with mocking eyes, and she realized he had seen through her ruse, but for the moment he was prepared to play along. She busied herself collecting the dirty plates from the table, and in their clatter, she asked: 'Did you not have – any children from this marriage?'

'No.' His reply was brief and uncompromising.

Ryan licked her lips. 'How – how long did it last?'

'Do you mean – how long were we married before she died?'

'What else could I mean?' Ryan was confused.

'Julia and I separated within two years. The marriage was seven years old when she died.'

'I see.' But of course, she didn't.

Alain pushed back his chair then and got to his feet. 'Is that all?'

Ryan looked up at him impatiently. 'You've made it seem like an intrusion!' she exclaimed.

He shrugged. 'I'm sorry.'

'No, you're not. You must know that two people don't marry for no good reason – that a separation can be caused by any number of things.'

'I do. But if you expect me to unburden myself to you, then I am afraid I have to disappoint you yet again. I am prepared to accept that you should know the facts of my previous marriage. The intimate details need not – *do* not concern you.' And with these words he turned and left her.

Christmas morning dawned bright and clear. Down the valley the church bells were ringing their greeting and Ryan realized with a sense of conscience that it was the first Christmas she had not attended the midnight service at the church.

But since their conversation on the day before Christmas Eve, Alain had seemed totally unapproachable, and she had not presumed to ask him whether he was going to attend the midnight Mass at St. Augustine's. She expected he had. Since their marriage, she had been aware of his leaving the house very early on Sunday mornings and returning long before she had prepared breakfast. Her own attendances had been few and far between, coming as she did from a primarily Protestant background, and in her aunt's house church attendances had not seemed so important. Daily she had expected the Abbé to reproach her tardy behaviour, but perhaps Alain had asked him to give her time to get used to their ways. What she did find hard to accept was that a man who so obviously believed in God and the power of the church should be prepared to enter into so empty a relationship as their marriage seemed to be.

A glance at her watch told her it was after eight o'clock and with a little sigh she slid out of bed. The night before, she had stuffed the turkey which Alain had provided at her instigation and she intended to prepare a truly English Christmas dinner. He had killed the bird a week ago, but she had gone up to her room and covered her ears to avoid the dreadful squawking that had gone on beforehand.

Now she left her room and entered the bathroom, rinsed her face and hands, scrubbed her teeth, and returned to get dressed. The door of Alain's room was closed, but that did not mean he was still in bed.

She put on the cream skirt and red shirt she had worn to go to Anciens that day. It was Christmas after all, and just because there was to be no especial celebration it did not mean that she had to behave exactly as on every other day. Besides, she felt like making herself look attractive, and a checked apron would guard against any splashes of grease.

Alain was invariably up before she was, with the fire already burning in the grate. But this morning there was no sign of him and the ashes of the previous nights fire were cold and uninviting. The kitchen was cold, too, colder than Ryan had ever felt it, and she shivered as she knelt to riddle out the coals. An unwelcome feeling of depression swept over her. Why was Alain absent today of all days?

And then she chided herself. Why not, after all? Most mornings he was up and it was only natural that occasionally he deserved a rest. But another thought struck her. What if he wasn't here? What if he had spent the night elsewhere and not yet returned?

She tipped the ashes on to an old newspaper, trying not to think about Alain's activities. She rolled more newspaper up and pushed it on to the coals that remained in the grate, added sticks and set a match to it. In no time the flames licked hungrily round the sticks and she added more fuel as the fire gathered strength. The warmth licked about her, too, and her fingers tingled with returning feeling.

Then she got to her feet and carried the ashes out to the bin. A damp rain moistened her cheeks, and the wind

80

whistled eerily through the eaves. It was a relief to get back inside again, to the cheery warmth of the now blazing fire.

By the time she had boiled the kettle and made tea, she was feeling a little less distrait. It didn't matter to her where Alain was or what he was doing, she told herself fiercely. A scratching at the door admitted the cat and Tabithe, who had gradually come to appreciate Ryan's contribution to her welfare, rubbed against her legs comfortingly. The appearance of the cat mewing for her breakfast reminded Ryan that she still had the turkey to attend to, and she lit the oven and carried the bird from the larder before sitting down to a cup of tea.

When the bird was satisfactorily installed in the oven out of reach of the hungry Tabithe, Ryan poured herself some tea and swallowed the reviving beverage with real enjoyment. Then, as she was pouring herself a second cup, the kitchen door opened and Alain appeared.

He had obviously just got up, for he had not troubled to shave and there was a stubbly growth of beard on his chin. In dark corded pants and a navy blue shirt which he was fastening as he came in, he looked sensual and disturbingly masculine, and her stomach muscles contracted alarmingly.

Raking a hand through his hair, he said: 'My God, Ryan, I am sorry! I overslept.' A reluctant smile tugged at the corners of his mouth. 'On Christmas morning, too. I expect my name is mud!'

Ryan found herself smiling in return, but whether that was in relief that he had actually been in bed and not out with someone else, she could not be sure. 'I – I – it's all right,' she stammered.

'No, it is not.' He closed the door behind him and scraped his fingers over his chin. 'I did not even stop to shave. I thought – I hoped that perhaps you had overslept, too.'

Ryan shook her head half apologetically. 'Er – would

you like some tea?'

She made to get another cup from the dresser, but he forestalled her. 'In a moment,' he said, standing between her and the tall wooden kitchen sideboard. 'First of all, I may be allowed to wish you a very happy Christmas, Ryan, and present you with this small token of my appreciation.' And to her complete and utter astonishment, he produced a small, gift-wrapped parcel from his pocket and put it into her hand.

Ryan stared at the package incredulously. Only in her wildest dreams had she imagined he might indeed buy her something. Not even when she had bought the bottle of after-shaving lotion had she really expected him to have a present for her.

'I – I don't know what to say,' she murmured.

'Open it. See if you like it,' he directed gently.

Ryan stripped off the gaily coloured wrapping paper with trembling fingers. It was a very small parcel; she imagined it must be a brooch or some earrings. But it was neither. When she eventually lifted the lid of the jewellers box it was to reveal a ring, a delicate cluster of diamonds on a fragile platinum band. She lifted her eyes to his in amazement, and he took the ring out of its velvet bed and slid it on to the finger that already bore the broad gold band of his possession. It fitted almost perfectly. Perhaps her fingers were a little slimmer than they had been when they got married, but it suited their slenderness and complemented its companion.

'As we had no time to buy an engagement ring, I thought perhaps you might like one,' he commented simply, twisting her hand so that the light from outside caught all the facets of the diamonds. 'It looks quite well, doesn't it?'

Ryan was speechless, and nodded wordlessly, realizing how puny the shaving lotion would seem after this.

'Well?' Alain expected her to say something, and she forced her lips to move.

82

'It – it's beautiful,' she breathed huskily.

'But do you like it?' he persisted.

'Of – of course I do.' She took a deep breath and looked up at him again. 'Thank you. Thank you, very much.' And on impulse she reached up and pressed a kiss to his cheek. His beard was rough against her lips, but she didn't mind, and for a disturbing moment her breasts were pressed against the muscular hardness of his chest. An unfamiliar weakness gripped her, and she swayed so that her hands reached automatically for his arm to steady herself. But before she could touch him, his hands closed on her upper arms, propelling her gently, but firmly, away from him.

As she controlled the ridiculous feeling of humiliation that filled her, he turned abruptly away, reaching for a cup and helping himself to some tea. By the time he had it poured and was drinking its creamy sweetness, Ryan was composed, her weakness hidden behind a mask of politeness.

Sliding the ring off her finger, she returned it to its box and then said: 'You – you shouldn't have done it, you know.'

His expression, too, was enigmatic. 'Why not?'

'It – it's too much – too expensive.'

'Allow me to decide what I can or cannot afford,' he returned rather curtly.

She shook her head. 'I have nothing so grand for you.'

Alain looked impatient. 'Do you suppose I expect you to give me a gift? The ring is in appreciation of the way you have settled down here. I realize it cannot have been easy for you, cut off as you are from all the things that were previously familiar. I am not good with words. The ring expresses my gratitude.'

Ryan wondered why his words diminished still further the pleasure she had initially felt when receiving the ring. In the beginning she had foolishly imagined it was a sign

83

that he was beginning to notice that he had a wife, but as events progressed it was becoming obvious that his motives had been entirely impersonal. She put the box containing the ring on the dresser and began to prepare breakfast. Christmas had made her fanciful. Had she forgotten that less than three months ago she had thought she despised Alain de Beaunes?

To her surprise, Alain offered to drive her down to Mass later in the morning. He had, he told her, attended the late night service on Christmas Eve, and that was why he had slept in that morning. But he was not averse to making a second communion, and Ryan was warmed by his concern for her spiritual welfare. Apparently in some things he did consider her feelings.

The Abbé was pleased to see her in the church and after the service was over he came to have a few words with them.

'I told Alain that you must attend on this most joyful of days, *chérie*,' he confided, thus again destroying Ryan's new-found warming towards her husband. 'Your first Christmas in the valley! May you have many many more.'

'Thank you, Father.' Ryan forced a smile, and then started when another voice said: 'Happy Christmas, Alain! Happy Christmas, Ryan!'

It was Vivienne Couvrier, vividly elegant in an emerald green trouser suit and a carelessly slung fox fur.

The old Abbé was included in the greeting and he smiled at her welcomingly. 'Good morning, *madame*. You look very well this dull morning. Obviously this cold weather does not trouble you. Myself, I find my old bones protesting.'

Vivienne accepted the priest's compliments charmingly, flattering him that he did not look a day older than fifty. The Abbé smiled and chuckled and other villagers stopped to share the joke. Vivienne regarded Alain and Ryan more thoughtfully.

'And what did St. Nicholas put into your stocking, Ryan?' she asked mockingly. 'Something nice, I hope.'

Ryan was sure she hoped nothing of the kind, and she wished she had worn her ring so that she could have thrust that under the other girl's nose. But she hadn't, so she merely said: 'I wasn't disappointed, *madame*. Were you?'

Vivienne hid any irritation she might have felt at this uninformative reply, and turned instead to Alain. 'And how about you, *mon cher*? Were you not disappointed also?'

Alain glanced fleetingly at his wife and then he answered: 'One should not expect, and then one is never disappointed.'

Vivienne laughed. His reply appeared to have pleased her. The Abbé spoke again, drawing his robes more closely about him. 'And now you must all come and join me in a glass of wine,' he said. 'It is a bottle from your vineyards, Alain. I do not think it will disappoint you.'

Ryan wished Alain would refuse, but of course he did not. Vivienne was obviously included in the invitation, and she had no desire to spend any longer in the older girl's company than was absolutely necessary. However, they could not disappoint the old priest, and she was obliged to follow his white-clad figure along the flagged path to his house, knowing that Alain and Vivienne were bringing up the rear.

Madame Villiers, the Abbé's housekeeper, greeted them warmly, smiling her introduction to Ryan. A fire warmed the tiny parlour, so much less formal than the parlour at the house, Ryan thought, and there was rich ruby wine, glowing in fine glasses. The atmosphere was almost festive, and Ryan relaxed, refusing to acknowledge that her husband was showing more interest in Vivienne than in herself.

'What are you going to do for the rest of the day, *madame*?' the Abbé asked Vivienne, distracting her attention from Alain.

Vivienne gave an impatient gesture. 'I am having lunch with the Columbes, Father,' she replied, 'and of course this afternoon I have to visit with my stepsons and their wives.' She twisted her lips. 'It is the custom, you understand.'

'Of course.' The priest nodded. 'But such customs are delightful, are they not? Having no children of your own, you must enjoy playing with the little ones. How many are there now? Six – or is it seven?'

'Eight, actually,' returned Vivienne, showing Ryan at least by her tone that she did not find the custom particularly enjoyable. She was all too eager to return her attention to Alain, but to Ryan's relief he announced that they must be going.

'Must you?' Vivienne was dismayed. 'But it's early yet, Alain.'

'Nevertheless, my wife has much still to prepare,' he answered evenly. 'We are to have a traditional English dinner, is that not right, Ryan?'

Ryan nodded, colouring a little under this unexpected scrutiny, and the Abbé clapped his hands. 'Charming, charming,' he exclaimed. 'Your wife can still be disconcerted by your attentions, Alain. And this after three months of marriage. It is enchanting, is it not, *madame*?' He turned once more to Vivienne.

But she chose to ignore his question, smiling instead at Alain, and saying: 'Perhaps you and your wife could come to dinner one evening, *chéri*. Shall we say – three days from now?'

Ryan's nerves tightened, but Alain merely frowned. 'Maybe. I will let you know, Vivienne. But thank you for the invitation.'

They said their good-byes to the priest and received his blessing, and then left the house, walking swiftly down the path to where Alain had left the station wagon. Ryan got quickly inside. The doors were not locked. There were no thieves in Bellaise.

Alain joined her, but before starting the engine he glanced sideways at her. 'Was that satisfactory?' he queried, and her eyes widened as she read the amusement in his.

'Was – what – all right?'

'My behaviour towards Madame Couvrier? You had no cause for complaint, did you?'

Ryan stared at him in bewilderment, hardly daring to believe that he could be teasing her about it. Then, half accepting it, she nodded slowly. 'You – you admit then that she is – well, attracted to you?'

'Vivienne likes men,' he agreed, turning the ignition. 'And men usually like her.'

Ryan sucked in her cheeks. 'Do you?'

'Of course.' His eyes mocked her again. 'I'm a man, aren't I?'

His reply was scarcely satisfactory, but it seemed it was the only one she was going to get. Nevertheless, his attempt at humour had succeeded in lightening her mood and she arrived back at the house feeling infinitely less downhearted.

She decided to serve dinner in the late afternoon and Alain was agreeable. 'It will give me time to check some figures that I need for the day after tomorrow,' he said, and she concealed the frustration she felt that he should feel the need to work today of all days.

However, she put the time to good use, preparing the vegetables and sauces she would need for the meal, and lighting the fire in the dining-room where she had decided they would eat for once. The dining-room table looked good covered with a white cloth and set with their cutlery and wine glasses, and the fire would soon diminish the chill that it presently possessed.

Satisfied that there was nothing more she could do for the moment, she went upstairs to take a bath. Then she dressed in the brown caftan, and turned critically before the dressing-table mirror. It looked just as attractive as it had done in the shop, but was it too formal for such an occasion? She sighed. What other opportunity might she have for wearing it? She decided to go ahead.

Downstairs again, the meal was nearing completion. There was no Christmas pudding, she had not thought of that; but she had made some mince pies and Marie's mother had presented her with a fruit cake.

On impulse, she lifted the small box from the dresser and put on the ring Alain had given her. It sparkled brilliantly in the light from the fire, and complemented the slenderness of her fingers. She was admiring it when Alain came into the room.

Unlike her, he had not changed, but the cream silk shirt and close-fitting suede trousers he had worn to attend Mass were not his normal, everyday attire. His eyes narrowed when they encountered Ryan's, and then travelled appraisingly down the length of her body.

Ryan stood very still, waiting for his opinion to be voiced, but all he said was: 'I'm hungry. Is the meal almost ready?'

She was so disappointed that she lost her temper. 'Yes. It's almost ready!' she snapped. 'It's just another meal, after all, isn't it? I might just as well have worn my jeans and sweater and served it in here, mightn't I?'

Alain's eyebrows lifted. 'Are we not eating in here?'

'No. No, we're not. I've laid the table in the dining-room for once, although I don't know why I bothered.'

She turned away, snatching up her apron and fumbling with the tapes around her waist. Tears blinded her eyes. She should have known better than to try and salvage something from such an impossible situation. Nothing had changed. Today was no different from any other day, and had she worn sackcloth and ashes he would not have noticed.

Then she started violently as fingers closed over her shoulders and warm breath fanned the nape of her neck.

She stiffened as he said: 'I am sorry, Ryan. I am insensitive. I should have realized that Christmas would remind you of other Christmases spent with your family—'

'Please let go of me!' She tried to struggle free of him. He could not have been more wrong, and the last thing she wanted was his sympathy. 'I have to see to the turkey . . .'

'Ryan, listen to me!' His fingers tightened. 'I am trying to tell you – I understand—'

'You don't! You can never understand!' she declared fiercely. 'Oh, let go of me!'

Impatience made him shake her and she lost her balance and fell back against him so that he released her shoulders to grasp her waist. And then, for a moment, he held her there against him, and she could feel the stirring pressure of his thighs. It was only for a moment, and after he had set her free and turned away to light a cheroot, she half wondered if she had imagined it. But one look at his taut face warned her she had not. However, his expression was not encouraging, and she hurriedly distracted herself by ladling out vegetables into serving dishes and setting the sauces to heat on the stove. As she did so, a curious weakness invaded her lower limbs at the recollection of his undoubted strength and virility, and she stole another glance at him. And as she met his frowning stare she had to acknowledge that she had not recoiled from the touch of his hard hands on her body.

The meal, surprisingly enough, was a success. Obviously determined to set aside all but the most immediate demands, Alain carved the turkey and complimented her on its taste and appearance. Everything was cooked to perfection, and had Ryan's own enjoyment not been eclipsed by her awareness of her own inner uncertainties she would have felt almost content. After the meal, she carried the dishes through to soak in the sink and then served coffee in the parlour.

She had intended to mention her plans for redecoration of this room to Alain today, but somehow she couldn't bring herself to talk of such mundane things. Besides, Alain, stretched out lazily in one of the armchairs beside the fire, made even its stiff lines look comfortable. He was having cognac with his coffee, and on impulse Ryan poured herself one. It was growing dark outside, and the wind whistling round the chimneys had a mournful air. But it was cosy in here, in the lamplight, the fireglow casting shadows on the ceiling.

Alain's eyes were half closed, but they opened wider as she poured the cognac, and after a moment he said: 'Don't drink too much of that. It's very potent.'

Ryan sipped the liquid in her glass experimentally, sitting opposite him in the other armchair. Its fiery heat spread throughout her body setting her toes and fingertips tingling.

Alain studied her for a moment, and then he said: 'The dinner was delicious. I would never have believed that English cooking could be so good. It always seems so dull and tasteless somehow.'

Ryan took another sip of her cognac. 'That is a story put about by jealous Frenchmen,' she replied, the spirit giving her confidence. 'But it was nice, wasn't it? There's an awful lot of washing up, though.'

'I'll help you with it later,' he offered, and she smiled at him through her lashes.

'Thank you. But I can manage. I'll do them later, as you say.' Then she sighed. 'Hmm, it is cosy in here, isn't it?' She examined her ring again which she had not taken off. 'Don't you think it looks rather attractive?' she asked, moving her fingers at the end of her outstretched arm.

'Very nice,' he agreed, and she swallowed some more of the cognac.

She sat for a while gazing into the fire, feeling the heat making her eyelids heavier. Alain had closed his eyes and in a little while she realized he was sleeping. She sighed again. Their first Christmas together. It had not been half so bad as she had at first expected. Alain's gift, and his teasing coming home from church, his attempt to placate her and that moment in his arms when she had felt the pulsing heat of his body . . .

She trembled and swallowed the remainder of the cognac in her glass to steady herself. What had it meant, that momentary weakening? And what would she have done if he had chosen to keep her there, in his arms? If he had twisted her around and laid his mouth against hers?

Her cheeks flamed, but the heat from the fire hid her blushes. Lifting the decanter, she poured herself some more cognac. Why not? she asked herself as her gaze flickered guiltily towards Alain. It was Christmas after all. Surely she was entitled to be reckless for once in the year.

She sipped the spirit slowly. It was curious how relaxed it made her feel. Not even the future – those nebulous Christmases stretching away into infinity seemed quite so depressing as they had done a few moments ago.

Alain had taken off his boots and his feet rested somewhere near hers. He had stretched out his long legs and looked completely at home and content. One hand rested over the arm of the chair, while the other was tucked into the low waistband of his pants. The silk shirt was unbuttoned at the neck to reveal the strong column of his throat and the angle of his head resting against the wing of the chair had tumbled the straight silvery fair hair across his forehead. In sleep he looked younger, more vulnerable, and she knew the desire to touch him, to awaken him, to make him aware of her.

Moving to her knees, she knelt at his feet, looking up at him. Impulsively, she allowed the fingers of one hand to curve round his ankle over the woollen texture of the socks he was wearing. Her action aroused no response, and she spread her fingers and pushed aside the offending material so that she touched the skin covering his shin bone. Looking down she saw that his flesh was not pale as she might have expected, but tanned like the rest of him, which proved he spent long hours in the heat of the sun, working alongside his employees. He moved then, restlessly, but she thought he must have imagined that Tabithe was stroking herself against his leg, for he didn't open his eyes.

Smiling to herself, Ryan shifted until her back was resting against his thighs, and drew a deep sighing breath. What was the matter with her? she asked herself. Why was she so restless suddenly? So discontented with their relationship? What did she want of this man who was her husband?

She pressed her lips unhappily together. She had never cared much for the company of the men she had known, and had certainly never felt any curiosity about the intimacies men and women could share. Indeed, at the time of her marriage, even the thought of entering into any kind of intimacy with a man had terrified her. But she was no longer terrified of Alain, and although at times she still felt she hated him, she had to admit to a certain curiosity about him. She shook her head impatiently. The cognac must be making her fanciful, she thought. How he would despise her if he knew what she was thinking.

He shifted again, adopting a more comfortable position in the stiff-backed chair, and Ryan froze as one hand brushed her shoulder before coming to rest in the hollow of her throat. Every breath she took made her even more aware of his fingers against her skin where the folds of the caftan fell away to a deep vee. She could not move without dislodging them.

But perhaps her trembling awareness, or maybe the unexpected softness of her skin against his disturbed his drowsing, for within seconds his eyes had opened and instantly assessed the situation. But he did not immediately withdraw his hand as she had expected. Instead, he held her startled gaze as she turned her head to look at him, and then deliberately allowed his fingers to probe the neckline of her gown and cup one small, rounded breast.

Ryan's breathing almost choked her. It all seemed to be happening in slow motion, almost like a dream. She knew it was up to her to draw back from the edge of the precipice she was stalking, but the pressure of his hand on her flesh was an aching delight. She wanted to press herself against him, she wanted to tear the clothes from her and let him caress every inch of burning flesh, but the wantonness of it all horrified her into action.

He didn't attempt to stop her when she scrambled to her feet, holding the neckline of the gown closely to her, but he turned on to his back and looked up at her with eyes that were frankly contemptuous. Ryan didn't know what to say – what could she say? – and yet something had to be said.

'I – I think we've both had too much cognac!' she got out at last, and his lips twisted cruelly.

'Do you?' He shook his head. 'Perhaps *you* have had too much cognac, *madame*. I have not.'

Ryan tried to calm her jerking nerves. 'Well – well, anyway—'

'Oh, in the name of *God*!' Alain dragged himself upright in the chair. 'You were asking for me to touch you, Ryan! I am not completely without experience of women, you know. I was interested to see how far you were prepared to go!'

Ryan gasped, 'What do you mean?'

He raised his eyes heavenward. 'Surely it is obvious. I am not unaware that for some time now you have been finding your claws, little cat. It had to happen. I was prepared for it. You will soon grow tired of sharpening them on me!'

'I don't know what you mean,' she persisted, and he rose to his feet, to tower over her, even in his socks.

'Have a care, little one. Men are unpredictable when aroused, and you are doing your best to arouse me. I do not altogether understand why, but I am prepared to put it down to your inexperience.'

Ryan felt humiliated. 'And I suppose I should feel grateful for that!'

'Perhaps,' he agreed evenly.

'And you had no part in my behaviour, of course!'

'Not willingly, no.'

'And what about before dinner?' Ryan spoke rashly, and then wished she could retract the words. But he would not let her. He caught her by the forearms as she would have turned away, and demanded: 'What about before dinner?'

Ryan's lips trembled. 'No – nothing.'

'That won't do.' His voice was ominously cold.

'Oh – oh, well – when you – when you tried to apologize.'

'And?'

If only she didn't have to go on! She licked her lips. 'When – when you held me in your arms, you – you—'

'Oh, I see.' His tone was derisive now. 'You thought—' He paused, and then continued: 'I am sorry to disappoint you, little one, but a man can be aroused by so many things.'

She tore herself away from him then and turning brought her hand hard against his lean, sardonic cheek. He tensed and for one awful moment she thought he was about to retaliate, but then without a word he turned and left the room. Some little time later, when Ryan was still standing in frozen misery by the fire, she heard the outer door slam, and realized he had left the house.

CHAPTER SIX

FOR three days Ryan scarcely saw Alain. He was out of the house most of the time, and when he was in it he kept out of her way. He breakfasted before she was up in the mornings, did not return for lunch, and their only contact was over the evening meal. Marie, who had returned to work two days after Christmas, knew that something was wrong, but Ryan refused even to discuss it with her.

On the third evening, however, when Alain came home to dinner, it was obvious that something was wrong with him. He had great difficulty in swallowing any of the delicious meat stew Ryan had prepared for him, and when she accidentally touched his flesh as she reached for his barely-touched plate she found his skin to be hot like fire. She realized he was running a temperature, that without doubt he had 'flu, or at least a severe attack of cold, but his grim countenance brooked no interference in what he would consider was his affair.

Still, she had to try, and rather awkwardly she said: 'Are you not feeling well, Alain?'

He raised haggard eyes to her face. 'And if I am not?'

'You should be in bed.' She hesitated nervously. 'You should see a doctor.'

'I will be all right, thank you.' His tone was sardonic. 'I am sorry I cannot appreciate your culinary expertise this evening, but to be quite honest – oh, *God*!'

He broke off suddenly, beads of sweat suddenly standing on his brow as a wave of nausea swept over him. He staggered to the sink, his lips twisted with self-derision, and lay there retching helplessly.

Ryan waited until the spasms had stopped and then, ignoring his weak attempts to thwart her, she dried his face with a towel and said quietly: 'You are going to bed. At once.'

He made no objection to this, and she tried to help him up the twisting staircase. But apart from the fact that he refused any help from her, his weight was such that she would have been of little use. However, once he was in his room and resting on the bed, she began to unbutton his shirt and unbuckle the belt of his pants.

'I can do it,' he muttered savagely, pushing her hands away, and she stood looking down at him worriedly. 'For God's sake, leave me alone!' he added. 'I tell you, I shall be all right.'

Ryan left him to get into bed, as much from her own embarrassment as from his annoyance, but she returned a few minutes later to find him lying shivering beneath the covers. There were no electric blankets here, she knew, but there were hot bottles, and now she sped down the stairs to fill as many as she could find.

There were four, but when she returned with them, Alain only scowled. 'Can you not leave me alone?' he demanded, refusing to let her draw back the covers to put them beside him.

'Do you want to get pneumonia?' she asked impatiently. 'Alain, be sensible! I only want to help you.'

She wrenched the covers back to his stomach and then caught her breath as the reason why she had never found any pyjamas of Alain's either in his room or in the washing became obvious to her. He didn't wear any.

Forcing a composure she was far from feeling, she pushed a bottle at either side of him, and then bent to put the others under the covers near his feet. She folded the covers round his shoulders again, and then ignoring his angry expression said: 'Do you have any pyjamas at all?'

'I doubt it.' He was unhelpful.

'But you need something,' she protested.

'Why? I have not needed anything for years.'

Ryan sighed and turned defeatedly away. 'I'm going to bring you some hot lemonade and some aspirins. Will you take them?'

'If it will keep you out of my room – yes,' he muttered ungratefully, breaking off as a spasm of coughing convulsed him.

Ryan went determinedly away. She was not going to be put off by his manner. Alain was a sick man, and it was up to her to ensure that he looked after himself.

She was relieved to see that when she looked in on her way to bed, he was sleeping. His breathing was a little ragged, but at least he was resting. She stood for several minutes in the doorway just looking at him, and then with a shrug of her shoulders she closed the door and went along the landing to her own room.

She was awakened in the early hours of the morning by the sound of him coughing. After only a moment's hesitation she slid out of bed, and pulling on her dressing-gown padded along the landing to his room. She opened the door tentatively, half afraid that he would shout at her for daring to enter his room at night, but she need not have worried. Alain was barely conscious, tossing and turning in the big bed, clearly suffering the effects of some kind of virus.

She approached the bed and laid a cool hand against his forehead. He was burning up, and yet when she touched him he shivered and gathered the covers more closely about him. She knew he was running a high fever and that somehow she had to stop him shivering.

Without stopping to think of what she was about to do, she went out of Alain's room and into the one that had been her father's. Apart from tidying the room regularly, she had not got around to clearing his things out, and she knew there were bound to be clean pyjamas in his drawers. She found a thick winceyette pair without any difficulty and carried them back into Alain's bedroom.

97

Then, with a determination she had not known she possessed, she began to help him into them.

He protested, but his condition was such that she doubted he was hardly aware of what she was doing. But *she* was aware, and she had to force herself not to stare at his strong muscular body.

The pyjamas were much too small, of course. The legs barely reached his shins, and the jacket would only fasten at the neck. Nevertheless, they served the purpose of covering his shoulders and back, and for a while he appeared to have stopped shivering.

She gathered the hot water bottles together and went downstairs to refill them. The kitchen clock revealed that it was half past two, and as the fire was dead the whole place felt chilled.

When she carried the bottles back upstairs, she found Alain had started shivering again. He was conscious, too, though there was little sign of recognition in his curious tawny eyes as she tucked the bottles back into position. She didn't know what else she could do, but it was certain that she could not go back to her room and leave him alone.

She left the room long enough to collect a pillow and a couple of blankets from her bed, and then returned to settle herself on a wicker armchair in the corner of the room for the rest of the night. Alain had closed his eyes again, so she extinguished all but one lamp and curled on to the chair.

It was not comfortable. Not even her candlewick dressing-gown cushioned her against the stiffness of the wickerwork, and it was an unyielding resting place. However, she must eventually have dozed, because she returned to consciousness with a start to hear Alain muttering restlessly in his sleep. He was twisting about again, dislodging the bedclothes, and she heard the words 'Louise' and 'shouldn't have done it' repeated several times.

Sliding off her chair, she approached the bed again and

looked down at him anxiously. He appeared to be delirious, and although the sweat was rolling off his body his chest felt cold. What could she do? she thought desperately. It was hours until morning when she was determined to call the doctor whatever Alain might say.

Then the solution presented itself. If she got into bed beside him, she could ensure that he kept the covers over him, and perhaps warm him a little with the heat from her body. She had read of people doing this sort of thing to keep warm in freezing temperatures, and although it was hardly that the room was cold.

Without taking off her dressing-gown, she drew back the bedclothes and slid beneath them. It was a wide bed, and he was lying in the middle of it. Trembling a little, she moved closer to him, and then stifled a gasp as feeling her presence he moved closer to her. She waited until he was still again and then drew the covers up round their ears, praying he would not wake up and be furious with her. It was strange. She feared his anger much more than anything else at this moment.

Gradually, warmed by her nearness and unable to dislodge the covers, Alain stopped his restless tossing and turning and slept more peaceably, only the laboured breathing bearing witness to the congestion in his lungs. Ryan lay awake long after he was still, but eventually she too must have slept because when she opened her eyes daylight was streaming through the cracks in the curtain.

For a moment she didn't know where she was. The room was unfamiliar and she couldn't understand what the unaccustomed weight across her legs might be. Someone's breathing was fanning her cheek, and she turned her head slightly on the pillow and saw Alain. He was still asleep, the dark lashes shadowing his cheeks, but the hectic colour had gone and he looked a little better. She lay motionless for a moment, wondering how she was to dislodge her legs from under one of his, and realized with

99

a sense of shock that she had no desire to move at all. She was warm and comfortable, and for a few minutes she indulged herself in a fantasy of imagining that theirs was a normal marriage, and when he woke up and found her there he would reach for her, and pull her close against him, so close that she could feel the hard strength of him, and then he would cover her mouth with his own, and caress her, and then . . . and then . . .

But her imaginings went no further. Apart from anything else, she had no experience of what happened next, and besides, if he did wake up and find her here he was more likely to throw her out of bed!

Inching her legs out from under his, she managed to edge her way to the side of the bed and slide out. She straightened her dressing gown, tugged impatient fingers through her hair, and looked down at him. She had the sense to realize that he was by no means fully recovered, and what he needed was antibiotics to fight the infection. And only a doctor could supply them.

She tiptoed out of the room and closed the door silently behind her before going to her own bedroom. Her watch told her it was after nine and she gasped in surprise. Marie would be here soon. And she wasn't even dressed.

As though to underline that point, there was a sudden knocking at the kitchen door downstairs. Without waiting to dress, Ryan flew down the stairs and opened the door cautiously, opening it wider when she found it was the village girl.

'Did you oversleep, *madame*?' she exclaimed in surprise, looking at Ryan's dressing-gown as she took off her coat. Then she saw the empty firegrate. 'And the *monsieur*?' Her eyes widened. 'He oversleeps, too?'

The mischievous twinkle which had now appeared in her eyes revealed all too clearly what she was thinking, but Ryan had to disillusion her. 'I did oversleep, yes,' she agreed, 'but Monsieur Alain is ill. I think it's the 'flu. Is there a doctor in the village?'

'Not in Bellaise, no, *madame*.' Marie was concerned. 'But in the next village – Lauviens. Would you like me to get him for you?'

'Could you?' Ryan stared at her hopefully. 'Oh, Marie, I wish you could. I can't drive, and I can't leave my – my husband.'

Marie began to put her coat on again. 'I will get my brother, Armand, to go to Lauviens, *madame*. He is not at work today either, but he will go. He has a thick head, you understand? Too much wine yesterday evening. Armand takes care of his health.' She made a face.

'That would be marvellous!' Ryan was so relieved she could have hugged her. 'Thank you, Marie.'

'It is nothing, *madame*.' Marie made a gesture of dismissal that was wholly continental in origin. 'I will be back very soon.'

After Marie had gone, Ryan quickly washed and dressed and tackled the fire while the kettle was boiling on the stove. She had just set a match to it when the kitchen door opened and Alain stood swaying on the threshold. He was dressed in the shirt and pants he had worn the day before, but he looked ghastly, and she got quickly to her feet.

'You shouldn't be out of bed—'

'You should have woken me,' he retorted thickly, brushing aside her concern. 'I have to be in Anciens at eleven o'clock, and I had intended seeing Gilbert before then.'

Ryan stared at him angrily. 'You know perfectly well that you won't be going anywhere!' she exclaimed. 'You're not fit to be on your feet, let alone behind the wheel of a car. You're running a raging temperature, you've been sick and shivery, and you're going back to bed.'

'Oh, am I?' He glared at her grimly. 'And who's going to make me?'

'I am.' She shook her head helplessly. 'Oh, Alain,

please! Don't take my word for it, feel your forehead, look at yourself! You're ill. Can't you see that?'

Alain grasped the door jamb for support. 'I'll be all right. Just give me a couple of aspirins as you did last night. I'll have a drop of cognac, too. That might warm me up.'

'No.' Ryan stood squarely before him, her hands on her hips. 'You're going back to bed, Alain. Do you want to collapse at the wheel, is that it? Do you need to prove what a hero you are?'

'Why, you—' He bit off an epithet and stared at her coldly. But she did not flinch, and he clenched his fists. 'You're not going to make me into some damned hypochondriac!' he muttered. 'I've not spent a day in bed since I came to Bellaise.'

'Perhaps you've never been so ill before,' she cried. 'Oh, Alain, I'm only thinking of you. Won't you do as I ask?'

He looked beyond her into the kitchen. 'Where's Marie? I heard her arrive some time ago.'

Ryan sighed. 'She – she's gone to do something for me. To – to get – something for me.'

'What?' His eyes narrowed.

'Does it matter?'

'It might. I – oh, *God*!' He broke off to cough rackingly, and the sound tore her nerves to shreds. 'For pity's sake, get me something to drink,' he gasped.

Ryan hesitated a moment and then with a helpless shrug went to pour him a glass of water. He grimaced as he tasted it, but it helped. By the time he had finished he was looking distinctly drawn and Ryan regarded him frustratedly.

'Well?' she said. 'Will you go back to bed now?'

Alain drew the back of his hand across his forehead, staring impatiently at the sweat he had removed. He sighed then and shook his head. 'Oh, God, I do not know. To go to bed is to give in to weakness.'

'No, it's not.' Ryan spread her hands. 'If you don't go back to bed, you'll be hospitalized within a week.'

Alain looked disbelievingly at her, but he did not contradict her. 'All right. All right,' he muttered flatly. 'I'll go back to bed. But I'm getting up this afternoon, do you understand?'

Ryan nodded, but she had the distinct feeling that Alain was being much too optimistic in his estimate. However, she knew better than to argue right then. She followed him up the stairs, and then halted in the doorway to his room when he said sardonically: 'Have you come to put my pyjamas on for me?'

Her cheeks burned. 'You were shivering last night,' she replied defensively.

'Was I?' He sank down on to the side of the bed and began taking off his boots and socks. 'So you put them on for me, did you?' He indicated the pyjamas strewn at the end of the bed.

'Yes.' Ryan twisted her hands together. 'So?'

He gave her a wry stare. 'I am not embarrassed. I have nothing to hide.'

'And – and will you put them on again?'

'If I must.' He nodded towards the wicker chair in the corner of the room and she saw the pillow and blankets she had forgotten to remove earlier. 'Did you sleep there?'

'As a matter of fact, yes.' Ryan shrugged. 'I was worried about you.' She turned away. 'I'll make some tea.'

Doctor Gervaise arrived about an hour later. Alain had had some tea but had refused anything to eat, and as he had asked for some aspirin she had given him some. She had not dared to tell him that she had sent for the doctor, and her fears were justified by his expression when she eventually ushered the doctor into his bedroom. His face mirrored his anger and frustration, but Doctor Gervaise ignored his mood and concentrated on his condition.

'Mmm,' he said at last, folding his stethoscope back into his bag. 'You've got influenza, *monsieur*. Your wife was right to send for me. Nowadays antibiotics can relieve the more painful symptoms somewhat. He produced a small bottle of tablets. 'I brought these with me just in case. I suggest you remain in bed until your temperature is normal, and take one of these every four hours.'

Alain made no protest, but his expression boded ill for after the doctor had left. Doctor Gervaise crossed the room to where Ryan was hovering near the doorway. 'I know I can rely on you to see that he takes these tablets, *madame*,' he said, with a slight smile. 'I will call back in two or three days. Your husband should be much improved by then.'

Ryan escorted the dapper little man downstairs and then returned with some reluctance to Alain's bedroom. He regarded her dourly from the pillows, and she said defensively: 'You were delirious last night. I – I had to send for him.'

Alain breathed heavily. 'Delirious?' He shook his head. 'I doubt you know what being delirious is like.'

'Well, anyway, you were very – restless.' She paused. 'Alain, you know I'm right. You're not fit to be up. A few days in bed will help you to get better that much quicker.'

'I do not intend to spend a few days in bed!' he retorted irritably. 'I admit – I was not fit to drive into Anciens this morning, but by tomorrow I shall be.'

Ryan made no demur. She gave him a drink to take the tablet that Doctor Gervaise had prescribed, and then went away. There was no point in arguing with him. Only time would prove which of them was right. At least he was warm and comfortable, and not running the risk of catching pneumonia as she had been so afraid he might.

Afraid?

The word stuck in her throat. Had she been *so* concerned about him? The state of his health was his concern, not hers. If he chose to run risks with it, it was not up to her to defy him. Why then did she have this intense capacity of anxiety for him, this feeling that motivated her protective instincts? It was foolish, and totally unwarranted. And he would not thank her for it.

Downstairs Marie was dusting in the hall. 'And how is Monsieur Alain?' she asked eagerly.

Ryan sighed. 'He will be all right, Marie. He's full of cold, and I think his head is probably throbbing, although he would never admit it. He has 'flu, as I suspected, but I'm afraid he does not make a good patient.'

Marie chuckled. 'What man does?'

Ryan was not sufficiently experienced to answer that, and leaving the girl she went into the kitchen.

At lunch time she produced a fluffy omelette to try and tempt him to eat something. At breakfast time he had not wanted any food, and even now she could see it was an effort to swallow the eggs. But he obviously wanted to recover his strength and didn't give up until more than half of the omelette had gone. Then he pushed the plate aside, and said: 'Lying here one does not get hungry,' in brusque tones.

Ryan let this go and picking up the tray, said: 'Would you like some fruit? Or cheese?'

She saw his instinctive shudder, which he tried to disguise, but he just said: 'No, thank you. Perhaps some coffee?'

'Of course.' Ryan carried the tray to the door. 'And another tablet, hmm?'

By evening, the antibiotics had begun to take effect and Alain slept more comfortably that night. Ryan looked in on her way to bed, but he was already asleep and in no need of her ministrations. When she got to bed, however, she found it less easy to relax. The memory of the previous night could not be dismissed so easily, and now that she had time to think she remembered the words he had muttered while he was unconscious.

She wondered who Louise could be. It was a common enough name, but it was not his wife's name, and she couldn't help the feeling of distaste it aroused within her. Was there some other woman in the village he went to see? Someone whose name was Louise? That aunt of her father's who had written to her had been called Louise, too, but as she was an old woman, and in any case Alain hardly knew her, he could not have been speaking of her.

Thinking of Louise Ferrier reminded her that she had still written no reply to her invitation. No doubt the old lady would consider her extremely rude not even answering her letter, but Alain's attitude had been such that she had postponed making any decision. Now she realized that she would have to write, if only to thank her for her letter, and offer some possibility of meeting her some time in the future.

She heaved a sigh and rolled on to her stomach. A trip to Paris sounded an exciting possibility, but not alone. Besides, how could she go and stay with someone she did not even know?

Thrusting all thoughts of Louise Ferrier aside, she tried to sleep, but it was not easy. What else was it Alain had said? Something about not having done something? That was it. He had said 'shouldn't have done it' several times. But what did it mean? And what had this to do with the unknown Louise? It was all a puzzle and one which she could hardly ask Alain to solve without sounding as though she was prying.

The next morning Marie did not turn up for work, and midway through the morning a young man, whom Ryan took to be one of her brothers, arrived to say that she was not feeling well and wouldn't be coming at all that day. Ryan was disappointed. She had several things she wanted from the store in the village, and she had hoped to leave Marie in charge while she went down. Alain had obviously tried to get up that morning without her knowledge; his shaving tackle had been left strewn across the shelf in the bathroom, but weakness must have driven him back to bed, because his attitude towards Ryan was rather aggrieved, as though he blamed her for his condition. She didn't like leaving him alone, anyway, and Marie's absence posed a problem.

It was solved at lunchtime by the arrival of the Abbé. Ryan had not seen him since Christmas morning, but she guessed he had encountered Alain about the village. He explained on arrival that he had just learned that Alain was ill, and Ryan welcomed him eagerly. Lunch was almost ready, she said as she showed him up the stairs, and she would be delighted if he would join them.

Alain was dozing when they entered his room, but the sound of their voices must have disturbed him because he opened his eyes at once and frowned at them.

'Now, my friend,' exclaimed the old priest warmly. 'What is this? You confined to your bed? I never would have believed it!'

Ryan raised her eyes heavenward. What a thing to say, she thought angrily. Surely he must know how Alain would react to that!

But, to her surprise, Alain took it all very amiably. He levered himself up on the pillows, and said: 'Why not? I have a built-in nurse to look after me, you know.'

The priest chuckled as he looked at Ryan. 'I see what you mean.' He seated himself on the side of the bed. 'But tell me seriously, how are you feeling?'

Ryan hesitated in the doorway. 'Er – would you like me to serve your lunch up here, Father?' she asked awkwardly, and the priest looked questioningly at Alain.

'Yes, by all means. Join me,' said Alain, coughing into his handkerchief. 'That is, if you're prepared to risk my germs. I should appreciate a little conversation.'

His mocking stare accompanied Ryan as she went out the door and down the stairs. He was determined to irritate her, one way or the other, she thought indignantly. What did he mean – he would appreciate some conversation? He had never shown any desire to talk to her. And all that about risking his germs – it was intended to upset her. And what was most annoying of all was that he had succeeded.

Nevertheless, the priest's presence enabled Ryan to leave the house after lunch and walk down the winding track to the village. It was good to be out in the air again, and she thrust her hands into the pockets of her camel coat, and flexed her toes in the knee-length suede boots. She had left her hair loose and by the time she reached the store it was a tangled skein of chestnut silk about her flushed cheeks. She was completely unaware of it, but she had never looked lovelier than she did as she entered the shop, and the young man turning away from the counter at her entrance caught his breath in surprise.

'*Excusez-moi, mademoiselle*,' he said, as he brushed past her in the narrow confines between the counters, and he spoke with such an obviously English accent that Ryan was brought up short. Almost on impulse, she burst out: 'You're English!' in that language.

The young man halted and looked back at her. He was rather an attractive young man with dark hair and boyish features. He was about medium height, and slenderly built. Not a lot taller than she was, in fact.

'Yes, *mademoiselle*,' he agreed slowly. Then: 'Are you?'

She smiled. 'Partly. I was brought up in England, but – but I live here now.' She glanced behind her and realized that Madame Caron, the *marchande*, was listening to their exchange with undisguised interest, and coloured slightly. 'I – er – it's so nice to hear an English voice again.'

The young man clearly thought so, too. 'I've just arrived in Bellaise,' he told her, ignoring Madame Caron, who probably couldn't understand what they were saying anyway. 'I'm to teach at the school here. English, I should explain,' he added humorously.

Ryan nodded. 'I'd heard someone was coming.'

'My name is Howard, David Howard. What's yours?'

Ryan glanced round again. 'Fe – I mean – de Beaunes, Ryan de Beaunes.'

'Hello, Ryan.'

'Hello, David.'

He shifted the bag of groceries he was carrying from one arm to the other. 'So where do you live? We must meet up again – two aliens in a foreign country, all that jazz.'

'Hardly that as far as I'm concerned,' she murmured uncomfortably. 'But – well, yes. I would like to talk to you again.'

'So where do you live? Do your parents live in Bell-aise?'

Ryan licked her lips. 'My – my parents are dead. I – I'm married, David. I live with my husband.'

His mouth dropped open. 'Oh, God, I'm sorry!' He stared at her apologetically. 'Here I've been rabbiting on, and you aren't at all interested.'

'Oh, no,' she interrupted him. 'Really, I am.' She broke off awkwardly. 'No, what I mean to say is – you must come to dinner some time. With – with my husband and me.'

'Well, thanks, I'd appreciate that. I've got a couple of rooms in the village, a sort of bed-sit, I suppose you'd call it. It's not big enough to be called a flat, but I'll make it home.' He sighed. 'I must be going. I only arrived two days ago, and the place is still like a tip. I have to get everything straight before I start work.'

Ryan nodded. 'Good luck – with the new job, I mean.'

David smiled, nodding. 'I'll need it. Be seeing you.'

'Yes.' Ryan made no positive invitation. ' 'Bye.'

In the silence that followed the jangling of the small bell that preceded and succeeded every movement of the door, she looked across at Madame Caron.

'The young man – he's a friend of yours?' inquired the shopkeeper curiously.

Ryan gasped. 'Heavens, no,' she exclaimed in English, and then shaking her head reverted to her father's tongue. 'No, *madame*, just a fellow countryman, that's all.'

CHAPTER SEVEN

MARIE returned to work the following morning and almost before she could get her coat off Ryan could tell that she was excited about something.

'Oh, *madame*,' she exclaimed, beaming at Ryan. 'Is it not exciting that Monsieur 'oward should be a friend of yours?'

Ryan stared at her in astonishment. 'Monsieur Howard – a friend of mine? Whatever are you talking about?'

Marie looked at her coyly out of the corners of her eyes. 'You do not have to pretend with me, *madame*. I will say nothing if you do not want me to. But you cannot deny that it looks quite a coincidence, does it not?'

'It isn't a coincidence at all!' retorted Ryan, getting angry. 'Monsieur Howard is not a friend of mine. I hardly know the man. I met him for the first time yesterday. If anyone has told you differently then they're lying!'

'Oh, surely not, *madame*.' Marie looked a little troubled now. 'Madame Caron – she told my mother—'

'—that I was talking to Monsieur Howard in her shop, is that it?' Ryan demanded.

'Yes, *madame*.'

'I see.' Ryan heaved a sigh. 'I might have known. Can nothing happen in this village without everyone knowing about it? Good lord, we were just exchanging greetings as people do who are foreigners together in another country.'

'But you are not a foreigner, *madame*! You are the wife of Monsieur de Beaunes—'

'I know that!' Ryan made an exasperated gesture. 'But I did live in England all my life until I came here, and David Howard is English, and – oh, what are you looking at me like that for?' She took an impatient step forward, and then something – some instinct – made her glance round. Alain was standing in the doorway to the hall, supporting himself against the doorpost. He was dressed in close-fitting corded pants and a thick black sweater, and although his face was pale, his eyes were glittering and alert. 'I – how – how long have you been standing there?' she faltered. 'You shouldn't be out of bed!'

'Obviously not.' His voice was cold. His gaze flicked to Marie. 'Have you nothing better to do than to stand here gossiping?'

Marie gasped and dropped a nervous curtsey. 'I – of course, *monsieur*. I am sorry, *monsieur*. Excuse me, *monsier*.' And she brushed past him as he stood aside to allow her to hurry out of the kitchen and up the stairs.

Then Alain entered the room and closed the door uncompromisingly behind him. 'Who is David Howard?' he demanded harshly.

Ryan gathered her scattered wits. 'Did you have to speak so curtly to Marie?' she asked, not answering his question.

'Yes.' Alain was abrupt. 'I repeat – who is David Howard?'

Ryan sighed. 'He's the new English teacher at the school.'

'The new English teacher?' Alain's brows drew together in a scowl. 'I see. And he is a friend of yours?'

'No. That is – I hardly know the man.'

'You know his name.'

'Of course I know his name. He – he introduced himself.'

'Where did you meet this man?' He made it sound like an assignation.

'I didn't actually *meet* him. I bumped into him – in the village stores, yesterday afternoon.'

'While I was being entertained by the good father?' Alain's lips twisted.

'Well – yes, I suppose so.'

'And you did not know you were going to meet this man?'

'No!' She stared at him defensively. 'How could I? I'd never even met him before yesterday.'

'And yet you call him by his Christian name, no?'

Ryan was trembling by now, she couldn't help it, he was so cold and derisive. 'In England, one doesn't stand on ceremony,' she replied carefully. 'He – he asked my name, and I told him. I – I also told him I was married. Does that satisfy you?'

Alain walked to the hearth to stand staring down into the fire for a few moments. Then he looked at her again. 'It seems to me that you are singularly indiscreet.'

'What do you mean?'

He shrugged scornfully. 'First you cannot wait to relate the details of our relationship to the serving girl, and now you display such interest in this Englishman that you have the whole village speculating upon a possible romance.'

'Oh, that's ridiculous!' Ryan felt stupidly near to tears. 'You're exaggerating.'

'No, I am not. You heard what Marie said.'

'I gather you did, too,' she exclaimed bitterly. 'You were not supposed to hear. You should still be in bed.'

'So it would seem.' His eyes raked her contemptuously. 'I had forgotten how women like to gossip about their affairs.'

Ryan gasped, and then, drumming up anger to hide her humiliation, she said: 'I don't see how you could – in the circumstances!' her lips curling.

Now it was Alain's turn to look momentarily disconcerted. 'I presume you mean something by that remark?'

'Of course.' Ryan refused to draw back even though his manner was meancing. 'I imagine Vivienne talks about your affair all the time!'

Alain stared at her with dislike. 'I have warned you before, Ryan, do not tread into deeper waters than you can safely navigate. You speak carelessly. It is fortunate for you that I am a patient man, but even my patience is not inexhaustible.'

'Then stop saying such things,' Ryan burst out tremulously, and then completely shamed herself by breaking into violent weeping, covering her face with her hands so that she could not see the contempt in his.

But what happened next was as usual unpredictable. With a muffled expletive Alain covered the space between them, his hands sliding over her shoulders, drawing her unresistingly towards him. She felt her cheek pressed against the rough texture of his sweater, and her legs hard against the length of his. He spoke words of comfort in her ear, consoling her and apologizing for making her cry, but all Ryan was conscious of was the nearness of his lean hips, the strength in the arms encircling her, and the purely animal sensations of warmth and closeness and body scents. Involuntarily she moved against him, her arms sliding round his waist to draw him nearer, and at once he had released himself, propelling her away from him, holding her at arm's length. She thought there was a look of strain on his face which had not been there before, and his mockery had been replaced by grim concern.

'So,' he said at last, 'we will say no more about it. But I would suggest in future you give more thought to the interpretations which might be put on your actions.'

Ryan dried her eyes with the back of her hand. She was still very much in the grip of emotions she didn't altogether understand and she just wanted him to go away and leave her alone to compose herself. Then she saw the beads of sweat standing on his forehead, and anxiety overcame all other considerations.

'You're still running a temperature!' she exclaimed, looking at him worriedly. 'Why did you come downstairs? Why did you get dressed?'

Alain expelled his breath on a sigh. 'Ryan, there are things I have to do . . .'

'But not yet, surely! Can't this – this Gilbert Chauvin handle your affairs until you're well again?'

'Gilbert Chauvin is in the village. How do you propose I speak with him?'

'I could get him to come here. I'll go down – or Marie will go down and ask him to come up,' she corrected herself hastily.

Alain's expression was wry, although the strain of being so long on his feet after two days in bed was beginning to tell on him. 'I will drive down to the village myself and see him,' he essayed firmly, shaking his head as if to clear his vision. 'It will not take long—'

'You can't!' Ryan clenched her fists and stared at him impotently. 'Alain – please!' She glanced towards the windows. 'Look, it's starting to rain. You can't go out in the wet!'

Alain turned his attention to the windows where drops of water were starting to create a continual running pattern. Frustration gleamed in his eyes, and Ryan pressed home her advantage.

'Let Marie go and see Gilbert Chauvin when she goes home at lunch time,' she suggested.

Alain looked at her then, and his expression was grim. 'What are you trying to do to me?' he demanded. 'Make me a weakling? Rain has never stopped me from doing anything.'

Ryan hesitated. Then she said: 'But you didn't have a wife to care about you before!'

His eyes narrowed. 'And do I now? Have a wife who cares about me, I mean?'

Ryan coloured, and unable to sustain the initiative, said unsteadily: 'I – I'd care about anyone who seemed determined to do something to undermine his recovery.'

'I see.'

Alain flexed his shoulder muscles wearily, and then crossed the room to pull on his leather coat. Ryan stared at him aghast. 'Where are you going?'

'You know where I am going,' he replied evenly. 'Make me some coffee. I will be back in fifteen minutes.'

'But – but – you can't—'

But he could. He was gone.

It was almost an hour before Alain returned and Ryan was almost frantic, sure he had crashed the car or collapsed at Gilbert Chauvin's house. She was on the point of putting on her outdoor clothes and going to look for him when the station wagon swung into the yard, and seconds later Alain himself entered the kitchen, shaking drops of water from his thick hair, Ryan turned on him, shaking with anger, not giving herself time to notice the look of exhaustion that had taken all the colour from his face and left him looking gaunt and weary.

'Where have you been all this time?' she demanded.

Alain took off his coat and assessed her thoroughly for a moment. Then he replied: 'You do ask a lot of unnecessary questions, do you not? I have been to the house of Gilbert Chauvin, as you suggested.'

'I didn't suggest you went there!' she denied hotly. 'You decided that!'

'All right, then. I have been to the house of Gilbert Chauvin, as I decided,' he agreed, sinking down wearily on to the settle beside the fire, resting his elbows on his knees and cupping his head in his hands.

Ryan's anger disappeared as swiftly as it had come. His attitude of defeat moved her as nothing else could have done. She went across to him and laid a hand on his shoulders, feeling the muscles grow taut beneath her fingers. 'I'm sorry,' she murmured uncomfortably. 'I'm sorry if I was bitchy, but I was so worried about you.'

Alain raised haggard eyes to her face. 'Would it please you to know that I feel like death?'

'*No!* No, of course, it wouldn't please me,' she protested vigorously. 'How – how do you feel?'

'*Terrible!*'

Ryan withdrew her hand and twisted her fingers together. 'So what do you intend to do now?'

His faint smile was half resigned, half derisive. 'I shall go back to bed,' he answered on a sigh. '*How are the mighty fallen* – is not that what they say?'

After that incident Ryan found she had a much easier patient on her hands. He was still impatient at his confinement, of course, but he no longer seemed to blame her for his condition. On the contrary, he always made her feel he was glad to see her when she entered his bedroom, and several times she carried her meal upstairs and had it with him. Marie watched this growing relationship with unconcealed satisfaction, and Ryan eventually felt bound to tell her that her sly innuendoes were totally uncalled-for.

'Oh, but, *madame*,' protested Marie, her eyes twinkling, 'you cannot deceive me. I have seen the way you look at Monsieur Alain. It is not the way you used to look at him when you were first married. Now there is much softness – much tenderness – a desire that he should notice you—'

'I've never heard such rubbish!' exclaimed Ryan heatedly. 'If you've seen anything in my eyes then it's simply concern that he shouldn't do anything to hinder his recovery, that's all.'

Marie looked unconvinced. 'Why deny it, *madame*?' she asked, spreading her hands inconsequentially. 'There are many women in the village who would like to change places with you. Just because you are beginnimg to notice the satisfaction your husband's body could give to a woman there is nothing to be ashamed of.'

Ryan's cheeks were flaming. 'You seem to have noticed quite a lot yourself, Marie!' she declared curtly. 'And I think you're confusing love with – with lust!'

Marie dimpled. 'Without lust, what is love? The union between a man and a woman is a cold thing without desire.'

'Oh, go away and get on with your duties!' exclaimed Ryan frustratedly. 'I shall expect you to finish before you leave.'

'Yes, *madame*.'

Marie sauntered away and Ryan wondered whether she was being too familiar with the girl. She doubted that Vivienne Couvrier would permit such conversations with her staff. Vivienne Couvrier! Ryan wondered why her name had suddenly sprung to mind. And then she remembered. Marie had mentioned that there were women in the village who would like to change places with her. She had no doubts at all that Vivienne Couvrier fell into that category.

The New Year was born and soon after this Alain was able to come downstairs to his study and conduct his business affairs from there. Gilbert Chauvin was a frequent visitor to the house, and Ryan grew to like the rotund little Frenchman who paid her such outrageous compliments and treated Alain's impatience with such tolerance.

Within another week Alain was able to get out and about again, and although he maintained his amiable attitude towards Ryan, it wasn't the same. They no longer lingered over lunch together, talking about casual topics like books and films, comparing likes and dislikes of all manner of things. She had not learned a lot about his past at this time, but she had felt that they were beginning to know one another's minds. His return to normal changed all that, and when he began going out in the evenings again she wanted to curl up and die.

Of course, she didn't. But a certain withdrawal crept into her manner towards him again, and as though he was aware of it he became cool and withdrawn as before. Christmas, its events and casualties, might never have been, and she sometimes wondered whether she had imagined that night spent in his bed.

Towards the end of January Ryan was visiting the village one afternoon for supplies when she saw Alain's station wagon parked in the forecourt of the garage. It was the first time she had seen his car there, although she conceded that had he parked round the back she would never have noticed it. She had no need to read the broad sign which indicated: *Poste d'Essence, G. Couvrier, Propriétaire*, to know whose garage it was, and as though to emphasize the point Vivienne Couvrier emerged from the small office at that moment accompanied by Alain and another, younger man.

The last thing Ryan wanted just then was to be found observing his movements, and although anyone seeing her would no doubt find it strange that she did not stop to speak to her husband, she hurriedly pushed open the door of the village stores and effaced herself amongst the jumble of boxes and fixtures. Fortunately Madame Caron had been through the back of the shop, and when she appeared her attention was not drawn to what was going on across the street.

But walking home again, Ryan found herself filled with righteous indignation. How dared Alain parade his affair with Vivienne Couvrier for everyone to see? How could he humiliate her so, particularly after the way he had behaved over David Howard? She wondered how the Englishman was getting on now that school had started. She had intended asking Alain whether she might invite him to dinner one evening, but circumstances had always been against it. Now she wished she could see him and ask him. She would have done so there and then, in the heat of her anger, and to hell with what Alain would say.

She had intended making a chicken curry for dinner that evening, serving it on a bed of flaky rice, with a raspberry mousse to follow. But she was so angry with Alain that she decided he could make do with something far less exotic like omelette and chips. The raspberry mousse, which she had made earlier in the day with some raspberries taken from the freezer, she put to the back of the fridge, and she set the table instead with cheese and biscuits.

If she had expected some violent reaction from Alain to this plain repast, she was sadly disappointed. He arrived home as usual, soon after five, was closeted in his study until seven, and then emerged to wash and change before their evening meal. Even when he sat down to the meal, he was obviously absorbed with his own thoughts, and Ryan held her tongue with difficulty.

By the time they had reached the coffee stage, Ryan was really frustrated, and she set his coffee before him with such a force that she spilled at least a third of it into the saucer. But at least she succeeded in arousing his interest, although his eyes were enigmatic as he said: 'Is something wrong?'

Ryan slammed their dirty plates into the sink. 'What could be wrong?' she demanded sharply.

'That is what I want to know.' Alain studied her expression as she turned back to the table. 'The meal was very enjoyable. Is that what you want me to say?'

'Oh, was it?' Ryan put her hands on her hips. 'Well, I thought it was dull and boring! I had intended making a chicken curry, but after going down to the village this afternoon I decided I couldn't be bothered!'

Alain shrugged, getting to his feet to get his cheroots. 'I do not expect you to go to a great deal of trouble on my account, Ryan,' he stated, lighting one of the long narrow cigars he favoured. 'And it was quite pleasant for a change.'

'I'm so glad!'

Ryan was openly sarcastic, and Alain gave her a resigned stare. 'If you have something on your mind, Ryan, then tell me. All this verbal skirmishing is very childish.'

'Oh, is it?' He could not have said anything to hurt her more. 'How tiresome for you! But then I am a child, aren't I? A boring, tiresome adolescent, whose company you avoid at every opportunity.'

Alain inhaled deeply on the cheroot and then studied its glowing tip. 'I presume you imagine I did not see you this afternoon,' he commented dryly, 'scuttling into Madame Caron's like a frightened rabbit!'

Ryan's lips parted in astonishment. 'You – saw – me?'

'Of course.'

'And of course you didn't say anything to your – your companion!' Ryan's mouth was sulky.

'Would you have wanted me to? Would you have wanted me to say – Oh, look, Vivienne, there's my wife. Pretending she hasn't seen me! I think not.'

His statement had taken Ryan's initiative, and she hunched her shoulders moodily. 'Don't pretend you expected to see me!' she muttered. 'I have to walk down to the village if I want something. No doubt your precious Madame Couvrier has you for her chauffeur.'

Alain's mouth twitched. 'You are jealous. How amused Vivienne would be if she knew.'

Ryan's head jerked up. 'I am not jealous!' she denied furiously. 'And don't you dare to tell her that I am.'

'Then stop behaving as though you own me!' he retorted curtly.

Ryan turned back to the sink. *'Go to hell!'* she muttered, almost inaudibly, but not quite.

CHAPTER EIGHT

DURING the following days Ryan avoided speaking to her husband. She behaved normally, doing the housework, preparing the meals, but outside of the common courtesies she said little. If Alain noticed, he chose to ignore it, no doubt assuming that sooner or later she would come round, and it was left to Marie to comment on the dark lines around Ryan's eyes and the drooping curve of her mouth.

'I think you are unhappy, *madame*,' she said one day, as they were folding some sheets. 'Has Monsieur Alain been unkind to you?'

'Don't be silly, Marie.' Ryan couldn't bear the sympathy in the other girl's voice. 'Hold the sheets more firmly. You're creasing them.'

'You don't answer, but I know, *madame*.' Marie was not to be put off. 'I have seen the light go out of your eyes.'

'You're much too fanciful, Marie.' Ryan laid the folded sheet over the airer. 'How's that brother of yours these days? Armand? Was that his name?'

'Armand is all right.' Marie shrugged inconsequentially. 'He is getting married soon.'

'Married?' Ryan was glad to have something else to think about. 'But he's only young, isn't he?'

'He's eighteen, *madame*. Old enough to father the child that Brigitte Toulouse is carrying.'

Ryan caught her breath. 'Oh! Oh, I see.' She made a helpless gesture. 'And how old is – Brigitte?'

'Seventeen, *madame*.' Marie's eyes twinkled at Ryan's expression. 'Do not feel sorry for her, *madame*. She has wanted Armand since he was – oh, fourteen, fifteen.' She smiled. 'He has only done what she wanted after all.'

Ryan turned away. She still couldn't get over the embarrassment of talking about such *intimate* things. To think that Brigitte – and Marie – and no doubt lots of other girls in the village knew everything there was to know about the relationship between a man and a woman, while she, married over three months, knew no more now than she had ever done. She tried to imagine how she would feel taking off her clothes in front of Alain and found the prospect so disturbing she had to abandon it.

Still, she had thought that their conversation about Marie's brother had successfully distracted the other girl's attention from Ryan's own affairs. Two days later, however, she had reason to doubt this.

It was another wet day and Alain had run Marie down to the village in the station wagon at lunchtime instead of allowing her to get soaked. After lunch, he had said he had to go into Anciens and as he had not invited Ryan to go with him she faced a miserable afternoon. The weather reflected her mood and she was pleasantly surprised when someone came knocking at the front door. No one she knew ever used the heavy oaken door that faced the sweep of the valley and although she was a little anxious about opening her door to strangers, curiosity overcame caution.

To her astonishment, David Howard stood sheltering under the canopy, and grinned with relief when he recognized her. His mackintosh was dripping with rain water, and his dark hair was plastered to his head. He had obviously walked up from the village and Ryan stood aside almost automatically, inviting him inside.

'Thank goodness it was the right house!' he exclaimed, shedding his mackintosh. 'What an afternoon!'

'Yes.' Ryan endeavoured to gather her scattered wits. 'I – er – won't you come through to the kitchen? It's warmer in there.'

'Thanks.'

David followed her across the hall and as he did so

Ryan wondered what Alain would say when he found out about this. Then she shook her head impatiently. He didn't control her every movement. If she chose to have David here then he should not object.

David hung his mackintosh on the hook behind the kitchen door and warmed his hands at the fire. 'Mmm, this is much better.' He glanced round at her hovering near the table. 'Surprised to see me?'

Ryan hesitated. 'Shocked would be more the word,' she conceded honestly. 'How did you find out where I lived?'

'Oh, I've known where you lived for some time,' he replied, surprisingly. 'Your name is not unknown in the village, as you must be aware. But it took some courage to come up here uninvited.'

Ryan sighed. 'I'm sorry. I did intend inviting you for a meal, but my husband has been ill, and – well, I haven't had the time, I'm afraid.'

'That's okay. I know how it is. Look—' he indicated the settle, 'won't you sit down? Then I can sit down, too.'

Ryan nodded vigorously. 'Oh, yes, please do sit down. I'm sorry if I seem such a poor hostess, but we don't get a lot of visitors.'

'So I hear.'

Ryan frowned. 'Who did you hear that from?'

David looked embarrassed now. 'Oh – just around. Look, do sit down. You're making me nervous.'

'I'll make some coffee—'

'Later,' he insisted, and with a smile she subsided on to the seat beside the fire. David seated himself opposite, and then he said: 'Now, that's better, isn't it?'

Ryan nodded, looking down rather impatiently at her shirt and jeans. If she had known she might get company she would have changed into something more feminine. She had so few opportunities for dressing up.

Forcing her thoughts into less depressing channels, she said: 'And how have you settled down in Bellaise? Do you like working at the school?'

David shrugged. 'It's all right. It will be better when the summer comes. Right now my rooms are cold and a little damp, and after school at night there is little for me to do. I don't have transport, you see, and Bellaise offers little in the way of entertainment, as I'm sure you know.'

Ryan nodded. 'People make their own entertainment here.'

'Do you mean the number of children there are around?' he inquired dryly, and she chuckled.

'No, of course not. I mean – people knit, and sew, and read. And talk.' She paused, realizing with a sense of astonishment that she was not discontented with the absence of organized entertainment. 'Don't you do any reading?'

David nodded. 'Of course I do. If I didn't I think I'd go quietly mad! No, but don't you ever wish there was a cinema you could attend, or a concert you could listen to? What did you do in England before you came here?'

'I worked in a library, actually.'

'In London?'

'No. A small south coast town, Lynport.'

'Oh, yes, I know it. It's not far from Southampton, is it? Near enough to London for you to know the advantages of urban life.'

'I didn't like London much. I liked Lynport, it was all right. But I'm afraid I didn't particularly care for going out a lot.'

David looked intrigued. 'And now you live here – in Bellaise. It's some transformation, you have to admit.'

Ryan looked down at her hands. 'I like Bellaise.'

'Do you?' David studied her bent head. 'How did you meet your husband?'

Ryan coloured. 'I – my father introduced us.'

'Your father? Oh, yes, I remember. Your father's dead, isn't he?'

'Yes.' Ryan got to her feet. 'Would you like some coffee?'

David nodded, not deceived by her sudden activity. 'Your husband's quite a bit older than you are, isn't he?'

Ryan was filling the coffee percolator and pretended not to hear him, but he repeated the question and she had to agree, taking care to avoid his eyes.

'Yes. I've never met him, of course, but I've heard about him.'

Ryan poured cream from the fridge into a jug. 'Do you take sugar, Mr. Howard?'

'The name's David, and yes, I take sugar. What's the matter, Ryan? Don't you like talking about your husband?'

Ryan gasped. 'I think that's rather an impertinent thing to say!'

'Nevertheless, it's true.' David crossed one leg over the other, leaning back lazily. 'I should tell you, my rooms in the village are with a family called Cartier. Jeanne Cartier is the aunt of Marie Rideau who I believe works for you.'

Suddenly it was transparently clear. 'I see.' Ryan's fingers curled into her palms. 'And I suppose you have been listening to Marie's gossip?' she demanded angrily.

David sighed, and getting to his feet came towards her. 'Gossip doesn't have to be listened to. It's common knowledge that you and Alain de Beaunes are not happy together.'

'Oh! Is it?' Ryan's cheeks burned. 'Well, I'm afraid common knowledge is mistaken! Alain and I are perfectly happy. Our marriage could not be more successful.'

'Indeed?' David shook his head. 'That's not what I've heard.'

'I don't particularly care what you've heard,' Ryan retorted, clattering cups into saucers, and wishing that Marie was here so that she could tell her exactly what she thought of her.

David seemed to realize he had gone too far. With a deliberate effort, he changed the subject, and soon had her laughing over the difficulties of teaching the declensions of irregular English verbs to a class of restless children. He was an amusing character when he was not involving her in personal questions, and Ryan found herself warming to him again. He was English, after all, and she had kown that their marriage would sound an unsatisfactory arrangement to the people she had known back in England.

She found she was sorry when it was time for him to leave. It seemed so long since anyone had talked to her, really talked, that is, and when he asked if he could come again she agreed. As he was leaving, however, she caught his arm and said impulsively: 'Please – don't tell Marie that you've been here, will you? I mean, I should hate her to get the wrong idea.'

David nodded understandingly. 'There's no reason why I should tell Marie anything. I hardly know the girl.'

During the next few days, Ryan's spirits rose again. David's next visit was something to look forward to, something to think about when Alain buried his face in account books and spoke to her in monosyllables. She said nothing to Marie of her feelings, and although she had been tempted to dismiss the girl in spite of her friendship towards her, to have done so would have required explanations involving David Howard which she did not want to have to give. So things progressed more or less as normal, and only occasionally did she find Marie watching her rather speculatively. She guessed the other girl must find her change of mood surprising in the circumstances, but she parried her questions and Marie was forced to draw her own conclusions.

The following Tuesday Alain told her he would be going to Lyon the following day. He suggested rather offhandedly that she might like to accompany him, and as this was his first overture of friendship since their row over Vivienne Couvrier, Ryan was eager to accept. The possibility that this might have been an opportunity of seeing David Howard faded into insignificance beside the prospect of several hours spent in Alain's company.

But on Wednesday morning she awoke with a thumping headache and the sure knowledge that she did not feel well enough to go anywhere.

Alain, for once, was sympathetic. He felt her hot forehead with his cool brown fingers and cupped the nape of her neck, looking down at her doubtfully. Ryan was overwhelmingly conscious of a desire to move closer to him and beg him to stay with her, but she realized that to do so would invite his contempt and nothing else. So she suffered his probing gentleness in silence and succeeded in arousing his compassion.

'Would you prefer me not to go away today?' he asked, his voice unusually soft and concerned.

Ryan looked timidly up at him. 'And – and if I said yes?'

'Then I should not go,' he replied steadily. 'You are my wife. You cared for me when I was ill, and I could do no less for you.'

'Oh, I see.' Ryan drew abruptly away from him. What a fool she had been to expect anything else. 'Then – no. You go. I'll be fine. I shall probably spend the morning in bed and see how I feel this afternoon. It's just a headache, nothing serious.'

Alain stared at her impatiently. 'Now what did I say wrong?'

'Nothing.' Ryan shook her head. 'I'm – tense, that's all. Go on, you'll be late.'

Alain looked at her for a long disturbing minute and she felt every bone and muscle in her body expand under that brooding gaze. She had not dressed and the folds of her dressing-gown did little to disguise the swelling maturity beneath. These weeks of simple living and good

128

food had given her a roundness that went well with the supple lines of her body, the slender length of her legs. She found herself remembering Christmas, and the hardness of his hand upon her breast, and a faint sigh escaped her.

With a muffled ejaculation that was half protest, half desperation, he stepped close to her and bending his head covered her mouth with his own. The contact brought his hands to her waist, drawing her closer, and her senses swam as breathing ceased. When he finally let her go, he was as pale as she was, and there was a glitter of anger in his eyes. He didn't say a word, he merely snatched his leather coat from the peg and disappeared out of the door.

Because Ryan had expected to be going to Lyon with Alain, Marie did not come that morning. Ryan could not say she was disappointed. The last thing she needed right now was Marie's knowing eyes upon her. She felt as though the searing touch of Alain's mouth had left his brand upon her leaving her weak and vulnerable. Alone with her thoughts, a little of the fear she had once felt for him returned. As her blood cooled, so too did her senses, and she was aghast at what had happened. She felt sure that had she not practically invited him to do so Alain would never have done what he did, and like that time at Christmas he now blamed her for making him lose control. But Ryan did not completely comprehend the demands of her own body, or the temptations that made her yearn for a satisfaction she barely understood. She tried to summon up the dislike she had at first felt for him, the repulsion towards his intense masculinity – but it wouldn't come. The fears she felt towards him now stemmed from an inner knowledge of the power he could exert over her, and she began to understand that there were more dangerous weapons than purely physical force.

Eventually her aching head drove her back to bed, and several aspirins ensured several hours of unconsciousness.

She was sleeping soundly when the knocking came at the front door.

Struggling up out of a drugged slumber was not easy, and she stared at the clock for several minutes before its face swam into focus. Two o'clock, she read disbelievingly. It couldn't be two o'clock. It was daylight!

And then she remembered. It was two o'clock in the afternoon, and someone was knocking at the door. Had Alain returned and found he had not got his key? Was he knocking at the front door because he knew that she slept at the front of the house and was more likely to hear him, or was it someone else? The latter was infinitely more credible.

With a sigh she slid out of bed, dragging on her dressing-gown as she padded to the window. Opening it, she peered down to the porch below, and encountered David Howard's amused gaze. 'Oh – hello!'

'Well, well!' David commented dryly. 'Not up yet?' He shook his head reprovingly. 'This is hardly the image of the hard-working *vigneron*'s wife!'

Ryan smiled. Her headache was much improved in spite of the rude awakening, and it was quite a relief to have someone else to talk to. 'I wasn't very well this morning,' she explained. 'I had a headache. I've been getting some rest.'

'Oh! Sorry!' He lifted his shoulders dismissingly. 'And how do you feel now?'

'Much better, thank you.' She hesitated. 'Do you want to wait until I get dressed? Or are you in a hurry?'

'No hurry. I've got all afternoon. Take your time.'

Ryan paused only a moment longer and then drew in her head and closed the window. It didn't take long to rinse her face and hands and put on a cream shirt and red pleated skirt, and she was running the brush through her hair as she opened the door. 'Come in,' she invited rather breathlessly.

David observed her appearance admiringly. 'Well,

well!' he remarked once more. 'So you do have legs – and very attractive ones, I might add. I was beginning to wonder. I've only seen you in trousers so far.'

Ryan flushed. 'Did no one ever tell you that it's rude to make personal remarks?' she exclaimed, but she wasn't really angry. 'Come into the kitchen and I'll make some coffee. I'm starving. I haven't eaten a thing yet today.'

He followed her into the kitchen and then stopped, sniffing. 'Mmm, something smells delicious.'

Ryan nodded towards the stove. 'It's some chicken soup I made last night,' she explained. 'Do you want some?'

David approached the stove and lifted the lid of the saucepan. 'Well, well,' he said again. 'Such accomplishments in one so young!'

'Don't be sarcastic. And stop saying "well, well". It's irritating. Do you want some or don't you?'

'Let's say I shouldn't say no.'

Ryan shook her head goodhumouredly, and lighted the ring beneath the pan. Then she filled the percolator and set it to bubble. While she put out spoons and dishes and some of the long French bread she had bought in the village the day before, David perched on the corner of the table watching her.

'So?' he said. 'How are things?'

Ryan busied herself at the stove so he should not see her face. 'Fine,' she answered quickly. 'How are things with you?'

'Not so bad,' he shrugged. 'I'm going away this weekend, as a matter of fact.'

'Away? Back to England?'

'No.' He grinned. 'To the Alps – skiing.'

'Skiing?' Ryan was interested. 'I went skiing once. It was years ago now, with a party from the school.'

'Not so many years ago, surely,' he teased.

'Well – five or six.' She paused, thinking. 'We went to Davos. You know – in the Swiss Alps. It was great fun. I think two of the party went home with broken legs, and one of the teachers twisted her ankle.' She giggled reminiscently. 'I wasn't much good at it, I'm afraid, but it was marvellous to watch the experts. Are you an expert?'

'Me?' David grimaced. 'You must be joking. It's all I can do to remain upright.'

'Have you been before?'

'Yes, twice.'

'Then I don't believe you.' She turned to ladle the soup into their dishes. 'I expect you're being modest to make me feel better.'

'Don't you believe it.' He straddled a chair and began spooning soup into his mouth. 'Hmm, this is marvellous! My mother used to make home-made soup like this.'

'Used to?'

'Yes. She's dead now. My father married again a couple of years ago.'

'I'm sorry.'

'Don't be. She had cancer. It was a blessed relief for her. And my father was only fifty when he remarried, too young to spend the rest of his life alone.'

'You're very understanding. Not all children feel like that about their parents. They tend to be jealous of intruders.'

'Do they?' David lifted his shoulders indifferently. 'Were you?'

'Me?' She seated herself opposite him, looking surprised.

'Yes, you. I hear that your parents divorced when you were quite young.'

'Yes,' she conceded, looking down at her plate, 'they did. But neither of them remarried.'

'No?'

'No. My father had a heart condition and – and my mother – well, I don't think she was entirely cut out for marriage.'

'Why do you say that?'

'I don't know.' Ryan had never talked like this about her parents before. 'She refused to return to France when my father had to come back here to take charge of the vineyard. He was French, you see. She was English.'

'Yes, I heard the story.'

'I see.' She bit her lip. 'You've been listening to gossip again.'

'Not at all.' He sighed, looking across at her as he broke some bread from the roll. 'Ryan, I was curious about you. About how you came to be here. I asked questions.'

'From whom?' She was horrified.

'Oh, not from Marie, don't worry. From her aunt mostly. I wanted to know how you reacted when you discovered that Alain de Beaunes had inherited half your father's estate.'

Ryan caught her breath, pushing her scarcely touched food aside. 'I don't see what it has to do with you,' she exclaimed, feeling the sickness of anxiety stirring in her stomach.

'Ni moi non plus,' remarked a harsh voice from the doorway which led into the hall, and looking up Ryan stared in amazement at her husband.

'Alain ...' she murmured faintly. 'then, still speaking in English, she went on: 'I – I thought you were in Lyon.'

'Pas possible!' He advanced grimly into the room and his expression brought David to his feet, too, demonstrating only too well the enormous differences in their physiques. Alain towered over the younger man, his bulk blocking David's avenue of escape. He said: 'You are the teacher of English from the school, *oui*?' His eyes swept over the other man contemptuously. 'Might I ask what you are doing here?'

David licked his dry lips and looked helplessly at Ryan. 'He – he didn't know I was – ill,' she interposed swiftly. 'He came to see me.'

'A votre invitation?'

Ryan hesitated. '*Peut-être.*'

'*Qu'est-ce que c'est?*'

'Oh, come on,' David broke in nervously. 'There's no need for you to play the heavy father, *monsieur*. Ryan and I are friends, that's all. There's no harm in our relationship.'

'I did not say there was.' Alain's lips twisted as he turned to his wife. 'You are feeling better, *non*?'

Ryan nodded jerkily. 'M-much better.'

'*Bien.*' But Alain did not sound concerned.

'Where – where did you come from?' she burst out suddenly. 'I mean, you never use the – the other door.'

'I seldom use it, *non*,' Alain agreed coldly. '*Mais aujourd'hui . . .*' He shrugged. 'You would not deny me that right, I hope.'

'Of course not.' Ryan moved uncomfortably. 'Please, Alain, let's not lose our tempers. I – we – we were just having some soup. Would you like some?'

Alain surveyed the pair of them with cold dislike. '*Non, merci.*' He unbuttoned his leather jacket, flexing his shoulder muscles as though the journey he had just made had tired him more than he had expected. 'I am – glad you have not been – how do I say it? – neglected? – in my absence, *non*? Myself, I have – business – in the village. I bid you both *adieu*.'

He turned and walked back into the hall, closing the door behind him. Ryan waited only a few seconds, her fingertips pressed to her lips, and then she sped across the kitchen and into the hall. '*Alain?*'

He was opening the front door as she reached him and his expression was not encouraging. '*Oui?*'

Ryan lapsed back into French. 'Where are you going?'

'That is no concern of yours, but as it happens I have already told you – to the village.'

'Alain, please . . .' She put her hand on his arm. 'Don't go like this.'

'Like what? I have assured myself that you are well cared for, have I not? I have discharged my duties as a husband.'

'Alain, you don't understand—'

'What do I not understand?' He removed her fingers from his arm with a jerk. 'That you have been consoling yourself with this Englishman?' He uttered an imprecation. 'But you are wrong. I understand only too well.'

'David and I hardly know one another,' she protested.

'No?' Alain plainly did not believe her. 'Yet you are on Christian name terms, and he treats you as if he knows you very well indeed.'

'That's just his way. It means nothing. I think he feels responsible for me—'

'*Responsible for you!*'

'Oh, you're deliberately misunderstanding what I'm trying to say. He – he thinks I'm English—'

'But you are not.'

'I know, but . . . Oh, why are you doing this?'

'I am trying to keep my temper as you asked me,' retorted Alain fiercely. 'Do not tempt me to go back in there and give that young pup the thrashing of his life!'

Ryan moved her head helplessly from side to side. 'I – I wish you wouldn't be so – so—'

'Crude? Boorish? Barbaric?' He supplied the words with savage mockery. 'Yes, I am all those things, as you will discover.' He stepped outside. 'Go back and entertain your visitor, Ryan. I have better things to do than stand here arguing with you. Do not bother to wait up for me. I may be very late. Perhaps you will be able to persuade your *boy-friend* to stay for supper, hmm?'

And with these parting words he left her, striding away round the house to where the station wagon was standing on the road.

CHAPTER NINE

It was after midnight when Alain eventually came home, but Ryan was not in bed. She had got undressed earlier, but she had known it was useless trying to sleep until she knew he was safely home. Besides, she had justified herself by deciding that he might want some food or a hot drink when he got in, and it would give her an opportunity of explaining David's presence that afternoon.

She was sitting in the firelight when he came in, and he didn't immediately notice her. He was taking off his coat and unbuttoning his shirt, throwing his tie over the back of a chair. But inevitably he switched on the light and stared at her with something like hatred in his eyes.

'What in hell are you doing down here?' he demanded angrily. 'I thought I told you not to wait up.'

There were deep lines beside his mouth, and his tousled hair bore witness to the number of times he had raked his hands through it. Or did it? Ryan's stomach shrank at the thought that another woman might be responsible for his strained and weary appearance.

'I – I wanted to talk to you,' she managed carefully.

'To talk to me? At this time of night!' He swayed slightly as he swung round to indicate the clock and she realized he had been drinking. 'There's nothing to say.'

'There is.' Ryan rose to her feet, wrapping her candlewick dressing-gown closer about her. 'Alain, I am not involved – sexually involved – with David Howard.'

'No?'

'No.' She sighed. 'Do you believe me?'

'No.'

'Oh, Alain . . .'

'Do not "oh, Alain" me! I have been hearing some things about you myself this evening. My dear little wife

– who entertains other men while her husband is away!'

'That's not true!'

'Of course it's true.' Alain's mouth was a thin line. 'I caught you myself this afternoon.' He shook his head. 'To think I didn't go to Lyons because I was worried about you!' Derision twisted his lips. 'I only got as far as Anciens. I telephoned from there that I couldn't make the meeting I was supposed to attend.'

'Oh, Alain . . .'

'*Oh, Alain,*' he mimicked her contemptuously. 'What a fool I was!'

'Alain, I didn't know David would appear!'

'You must have had some idea. It's not the first time, is it?'

Ryan hesitated. 'There was – one – other occasion.'

'*One!*' He obviously thought she was lying.

'It's the truth. Honestly, Alain. Why should I lie? What I do means nothing to you.'

'What do you mean?' He took a few steps towards her.

She flushed, but stood her ground. 'What I say. You – you don't really care what I do. Except in as much as I am a possession of yours and therefore you feel you have the right to do all my thinking for me.'

His eyes narrowed, the heavy lids veiling his expression. 'Is that what you think?'

Ryan nodded. 'Well, I'm not permitted to question your movements, am I?'

'What movements are you referring to?'

Had she been more alert to his mood and less to his physical nearness, she would have detected the change in his voice, the menacing quality which had crept in behind the anger.

'Your – your relationship with – with Vivienne Couvrier.'

'You know nothing about my relationship with Vivienne Couvrier,' he stated, coming to stand in front of her. 'Do you?'

'I can guess!' she declared unsteadily.

'Oh, yes? And how far can your guessing take you?'

'I don't understand.' She looked up into his dark face.

'I mean – what experience have you – an *innocent* – in such matters?'

'Don't be *horrible*!'

'It is horrible to call you an innocent?'

'The way you said it – yes.' She looked away from him, concentrating on the toes of her slippers.

'How would you like me to say it, then?' he queried, and now she caught the threatening tone. Her head lifted a little, and she stared at the silver buckle of his belt.

'I don't think I want you to say anything more to me,' she stated, through stiff lips. 'But I am not a liar, whatever you may think.'

Alain began to unbutton his shirt, pulling it free of his pants. He rubbed his fingers over the hair-roughened skin of his chest. Then he captured one of her hands and drew it to his chest also, holding it there beneath his.

Immediately her senses stirred wildly, and her breathing quickened. She could feel the heavy beating of his heart beneath her palm and her eyes went automatically to his, wide and questioning.

'Alain . . .' she began uncertainly, shocked by the frank sensuality she saw there, but he merely shook his head and bent until his lips were caressing the skin of her neck just below one ear. 'Alain,' she said again, more huskily this time, and he slid his arms right round her, arching her body against his.

Her face was pressed against his chest now and she could feel his tongue seeking out the secret hollows at the nape of her neck. His breath was faintly scented with the sweetness of cognac, and his skin smelt of the talc he used after bathing. And something else . . . Something that she

138

eventually identified as oil ... Oil? For an instant her brain took over. Lubrication! The kind used in garages ...

She tore herself away from him, breathing rapidly, staring at him scornfully. 'Don't touch me!' she exclaimed furiously. 'Don't dare to lay your filthy hands on me! What's the matter? Didn't Vivienne come up to scratch this evening, or are you just intent on proving how virile you think you are? You came back here this afternoon casting aspersions on David and me, and then go out and spend the evening with your mistress! Just who do you think you are, Alain? Just what did you think you were doing just now?'

Alain regarded her in a way which, had she not been so incensed, would have demoralized her. Then he said: 'I was merely satisfying that need you have to feel that you're a woman.' He inclined his head. 'Obviously you've proved exactly the opposite!'

Ryan gasped, 'Are you saying – I invited – that?'

'Let us say you made no objection. Not – at least – until you had this crazy idea about Vivienne.'

'It's not crazy. I can smell the garage on you!' she declared bitterly.

His smile was derisive. 'And what do you think? That we lie down amongst the tools and lubricants? Oh, grow up, Ryan, for God's sake! Vivienne does not live at the garage, and even if she did, she is too fastidious to enter the workshops.'

Ryan took a step backward. Put like that it did sound ridiculous. 'Well, anyway, you can't deny you've been with her—'

'I don't intend to. I do not have to categorize my movements for you.'

'That's right,' she exclaimed. 'Bluff your way out of it.'

'I am not bluffing.' Alain's scowl was menacing. 'Go to bed, Ryan. You make me rather sick.'

Ryan stumbled to the door, eager to get out of his sight,

and crept up the stairs to her room. She was shivering, but the coldness came from within, not without. Her room had never seemed more bare, more unwelcoming, than it did at that moment, and she collapsed on to the bed, her shoulders shaking.

It seemed hours before she heard Alain making his way up to bed. His steps seemed more unsteady than before and she guessed he had been drinking downstairs. She heard him in the bathroom and then the slam as his bedroom door closed behind him.

For several minutes after the house had become silent she continued to remain motionless on the bed, and then she got up and walked restlessly about the room. Now that she had had time to think she was realizing how stupidly she had behaved. How on earth were they to sustain this marriage if she was to continually behave as if he owed allegiance to her? But her feelings towards him had changed, of that she had no doubts, and *jealousy* was her prime motivation.

With a sigh she opened her bedroom door and went along to the bathroom. When she came back, she unfastened her dressing-gown and was about to climb into bed when a slight movement in the corner of the room caught her eye. She turned her head slowly and saw two beady eyes staring at her in the darkness. Her skin went cold and yet moistened with sweat, and alarm feathered along her veins. What was it? A mouse? A *rat*? Oh, God, she thought sickly, let it not be a rat!

She groped for the lamp, but in her haste overturned it and the creature, whatever it was, scuttled across the floor. Stifling a scream, she wrenched open the door and flew along the passage to Alain's room, bursting in without knocking. The light was out, he was already in bed, but her activities must have aroused him because, as she switched on the light, he was already upright in the bed. He blinked at her coldly and said: 'Now what do you want?'

Ryan grasped the handle of the door like a lifeline, standing there quivering like a leaf. 'I – there – there's something in my room,' she got out convulsively. 'I – I think it might be – a – rat!'

Alain heaved a sigh and she averted her eyes as he swung his legs out of bed and pulled on the towelling robe lying at its foot. He brushed past her without a word and went along to her room while she stood there trembling, dreading his anger when he came back.

He came back silently and shrugged his shoulders. 'There's nothing there now. I'd hazard a guess that it was a mouse, not a rat. We don't get many rats around here. But I'll lay a trap for it tomorrow and see what happens.'

Ryan nodded, straightening, endeavouring to regain her composure. But her nightgown was no kind of covering, and coldness of one kind or another enveloped her.

Alain stood by his bed, regarding her steadily. 'Well?' he said. 'What are you waiting for?'

Ryan shook her head. 'N-nothing.' She looked at him. 'Alain, I – I know this is not the time or the place, but I'm sorry for what I said this evening—'

'Forget it.'

She half turned away. 'Good night, then.'

'Good night.' He was abrupt.

She took a step and then glanced round. 'Alain—'

'Oh, for pity's sake, Ryan, what are you trying to do to me?' His voice, thickened by the wine he had consumed, sent a thrill of apprehension along her spine. In a couple of strides he had reached her, his hands sliding round her waist and over her stomach, pressing her violently back against him. 'If this is what you want, why didn't you say so?' he muttered fiercely, and the full realization of what she was inviting hit her.

She struggled then, but it was a futile exercise against his strength. Besides, curiosity was fighting a battle with common sense inside her, and even her fear was no cer-

141

tain defence. He picked her up and carried her to the bed, extinguishing the light before shedding his robe. Ryan fought desperately then, as fear overcame all else, but he was determined to show her that there was no turning back, and her horror increased as waves of pain swept over her . . .

She lay awake long after his breathing had become deep and relaxed, and hatred for him filled her with the desire to hurt him as he had hurt her. She ached in every limb, and she knew there would be bruises on her body in the light of morning. And yet she made no move to go back to her own room. She told herself it was because she still feared her small nocturnal visitor, but if she was honest she had to admit that deep inside her she wanted to feel the satisfaction that Marie was always talking about. Who knows, she thought miserably, perhaps it would come. She could not believe that any woman could find satisfaction in the thing which had just happened to her, and she could only imagine that a sense of well-being might follow such an event. But no well-being ensued, just a sense of inadequacy, and eventually she slept.

She awakened in the grey light of early morning to feel Alain's lips caressing her neck and ears and she twisted desperately beneath his hands, trying to thrust him away. But his mouth sought and found hers. She was still half relaxed and sleepy, and his urgent lips awakened a response inside her which refused to be denied. Her protests died under his deliberate expertise and far from simply taking his satisfaction as he had done the night before in his anger, he seemed determined to give her the pleasure she had not known existed. Soon she was responding eagerly to his advances, winding her arms around his neck, pressing herself against him, uncaring of the pain she only half remembered.

'Ryan . . .' he murmured, half protestingly, 'Ryan, this is madness!' But it was a madness they were neither of them strong enough to withstand, and their union was as satisfying and pleasurable as Ryan could have desired. Afterwards she snuggled against him like a cat, falling asleep in his arms without care to the future.

She awakened in the middle of the morning to find sunlight slanting down on her through a crack in the curtains. She rolled over expectantly, but the bed was empty. Alain had gone, and only the yielding lethargy that lingered in her limbs bore witness to the fact that she was his wife now in every meaning of the word.

Reluctantly, she rose and bathed and dressed, and then went downstairs in something of a daze to find Marie making coffee at the stove. The sight of the other girl sobered her, particularly as Marie's smile had a knowing quality about it. But she could know nothing, Ryan told herself severely. Alain would never discuss what had happened with her, and it was up to her, Ryan, to behave naturally and not arouse comment.

'Good morning, *madame*.' Marie was polite. 'You are late.'

Ryan was unable to control her colour, but she did managed to control her voice. 'Er – where is my husband?' she inquired.

'Monsieur Alain left almost two hours ago, *madame*. It is nearly eleven o'clock. But he said you had had a – restless night, and that you should be permitted to sleep on. I have kept very quiet, *madame*.'

'Thank you.' Ryan hid her annoyance. 'And I do know what time it is.' She sighed, wondering why she had imagined that Alain might not leave before seeing her. 'I – er – I wasn't well enough to go to Lyon yesterday.'

'No, *madame*.' Marie turned back to the stove. 'Would you like some coffee?'

'Oh – yes. Yes, please.' Ryan endeavoured to speak calmly. 'That would be nice.' She glanced round. 'What have you been doing?'

143

'Monsieur Alain told me you had been frightened by a mouse in your bedroom last night, *madame*. I have set a trap there to catch it.' She poured steaming black coffee into a patterned earthenware beaker. 'There. Can I get you anything else?'

There was a note of challenge in her voice which Ryan could not ignore. It was obvious if Marie had been upstairs to set a trap she must know that Ryan had not spent the night in her own bed. She thought quickly, not really knowing whether she should say anything or not. Until Alain came home, until she had had the chance to discuss this new development in their relationship with him, she did not feel able to make any statements. Nevertheless it would have been cowardly not to say anything, so cupping the beaker between her fingers she said: 'I – I thought you just said my husband asked you not to disturb me?'

'To disturb you, *madame*?' Marie frowned, and Ryan's pulses quickened. 'Oh – oh, yes, I understand. You mean in the matter of setting the trap.' She smiled. 'Monsieur Alain explained that as you were nervous about it, he allowed you to sleep in his bed and he took yours.'

Ryan was glad she had the beaker to hold. So that was how Alain had explained it. She might have known he would not be stuck for an excuse. Now it was up to her to explain herself again.

'I – er – I just thought that fiddling about with mousetraps could be – awkward. Particularly if they unexpectedly sprang themselves.'

Marie shook her head. 'I was very careful, *madame*.' She paused. 'And are you feeling better today?'

'Better?' the word slipped out. 'Oh – yes, thank you, Marie.' She swallowed a mouthful of coffee. 'I suppose I'd better hurry up. I haven't even begun to think what we can have for lunch.'

'Monsieur Alain said to tell you that he would not be in for lunch, *madame*.'

'Not be in? Why not?' Ryan stared at her.

'He has gone to Lyon, *madame*. As he did not go yesterday he has gone today.'

Ryan could not have felt more shattered. That he should go to Lyon today of all days! Not only that, that he should not invite her to go with him!

'I see.' She managed the words with difficulty. 'There – there's no hurry then, is there?'

'No, *madame*.'

It was a curious day and not one Ryan would have liked to have gone through again. Marie left at lunchtime and the afternoon stretched ahead to infinity. Some sewing occupied the earlier part of the afternoon and later on she took a bath and washed her hair. She had no idea what time to expect Alain, so she made some meat and vegetable pasties which could be quickly heated under the grill, left a tossed salad in the fridge beside an apricot flan.

By eight o'clock she was ravenously hungry and helped herself to one of the pasties and a little salad. She was beginning to feel concerned about Alain and the emptiness inside her didn't help.

It was almost nine-thirty when the station wagon came into the yard, and by this time her nerves were taut as violin strings, and an awful feeling of foreboding was cooling her flesh. Alain came in without any apparent stress, gave her a slight smile and removed his coat. He washed his hands at the sink, and then drying them, said: 'Sorry I'm late, Ryan. I got held up. François Dupon insisted I stayed and ate with them. You haven't made anything special, have you?'

Ryan, who had been in the course of lighting the grill, immediately turned it off. 'Nothing special,' she replied, in a tight little voice.

Alain turned to her slowly. 'Marie told you I had gone to Lyon, didn't she?'

'Yes. Yes, of course.'

145

Ryan refused to look at him. In a cream shirt and cream suede pants he was disturbingly attractive to her, but in spite of her newly washed, silky soft hair, and the sinuous folds of the velvet caftan he seemed indifferent to her. She could hardly believe this was the same man who last night had made violent love to her and who, early this morning, had aroused in her the kind of feeling which until then she had only read about.

Alain came towards the fire and warmed his hands at the blaze. 'Have you had a good day?' he asked, seeking her eyes with his, but still she avoided him.

'I've had a – very quiet day.'

'No visitors?'

Her hackles rose. 'What is that supposed to mean?'

'Why, nothing. I wondered if the Abbé might have been up. He told me yesterday evening he would try to get up and see you.'

Ryan chewed her lower lip. 'No one came.'

Alain straightened, thrusting his thumbs into the low belt of his pants and surveying her appraisingly. 'You're looking particularly elegant this evening. You should wear long clothes more often. They suit you.'

Ryan raised her eyebrows but she didn't make any response. She was trying to gauge his mood. He seemed amiable enough, and certainly he was not trying to bait her as she had at first thought he was. But still this wasn't altogether like him. He was assuming a surface charm, behaving in a polite and civilized manner, and yet she sensed that underneath he was controlling emotions of a very different kind. But what emotions? What were his real feelings? She wished she knew.

She busied herself, tidying the unused plates away, putting the flan and salad back into the fridge, while he lit a cheroot and stood with his back to the fire, his expression brooding in repose. This was crazy, she told herself helplessly. After what had happened last night there had to be other things to say, other arrangements to make, but how could she presume to make them? Although she now knew herself to be in love with him, he had never, even in his most passionate moments, mentioned love to her, and it was not something she should necessarily expect from him. But surely things could not go on as they were . . . Could she stand that? And if not, could she stand to leave him?

At last, when there was nothing else for her to do, she came to stand beside the fire, too, praying that he would make some move towards her. He glanced at her averted face, and then throwing the stub of his cheroot into the flames, he said: 'Ryan, I have something to say to you.'

'Yes?' Her heart lifted and she looked up at him expectantly.

'Yes.' He sighed deeply. 'Ryan, when your father made his will and insisted on this – ridiculous condition, that of our getting married, I mean, he made no actual mention of where we were supposed to live.' He paused. 'What I'm saying is – well, to begin with it seemed reasonable that we should share this house, as it was here, and live as an ordinary married couple, except – except in one instance. Do you agree?'

Ryan pressed a hand to her churning stomach. 'Yes,' she managed faintly.

'Yes. Well, that was at the beginning, as I said.' He lifted his broad shoulders. 'Perhaps it was a foolish arrangement, but I thought—' He broke off. 'Anyway, what I am trying to say is this: there is no real reason why we should – share this house. I mean, your father doesn't lay down that stipulation. There's no earthly reason why you shouldn't leave here, go back to England if you want, make a home for yourself elsewhere.'

Ryan stared at him in horror. 'What are you saying?'

He shook his head impatiently. 'I was a fool ever to imagine we could live together without hurting one another,' he muttered. 'But I needed a housekeeper and you needed a home . . .'

Ryan felt sick. 'You – you still do. *I* still do,' she protested weakly.

'Yes, I know. But the situation has changed, hasn't it?'

'You mean – after last night . . .'

'Of course I mean after last night,' he exclaimed. 'Good God, I never imagined myself capable of – of seducing a child!'

'But I'm not a child,' she cried.

'All right.' His face was grim. 'You are not a child. But you are little more. You trusted me, and I betrayed that trust. I could say that I was not entirely to blame for what happened, that there are limits to my endurance, but that does not excuse me. I have little self-respect after last night. At least allow me to keep what little I have.'

'You make it sound – sordid—'

'It was sordid!' he declared coldly. 'Do you think I am proud of what I did?'

Ryan shook her head. 'I – I was to – to blame—'

Alain's expression contorted. 'For God's sake, Ryan,' he swore violently, 'let us be done with it.' There was no trace of that surface tolerance now. 'I warned you once about trying your claws on me. What happened was the direct result of too much wine and too little self-control!'

Ryan pressed her palms to her cheeks. 'But I wanted you – to – to make love to me,' she breathed.

He stiffened. 'I refuse to listen to such sentimentality. There was no love in what happened, just a physical satiation of the senses.'

Ryan could not believe he was saying these words. And yet wasn't this exactly what she had been afraid of? But she had to say one thing more. 'And did I?' she asked. 'Satisfy you, I mean?'

Alain glared down at her. 'What do you think?'

'I – I think I did.'

He stared at her for a moment longer and a trace of

what had kindled between them the night before showed in his eyes. It was only a fleeting glimpse, but it was a faint ray of hope in a suddenly dark world. Then he turned abruptly away, and said: 'How much money do you think you will need to find yourself an apartment and furnish it to your liking?'

Ryan caught her breath, and for a moment the pain of what he was saying paralysed her. Then suddenly she was not afraid any longer. After all, this was her house as much as it was his.

'I shan't be leaving,' she stated quietly.

He swung round on her. 'What do you mean?'

'Just what I say. I shan't be leaving. I'm staying here. This is my home.'

'Do you realize what you are saying? I *want* you to leave.'

'And I don't want to go.'

Alain's eyes were hard. 'I can make life pretty unpleasant if you stay.'

She shook her head. 'I'll have to chance that.'

'*Ryan!*' He clenched his fists impotently. 'Ryan, for God's sake – do as I ask, please!'

'No.'

He drew an unsteady breath. 'Then I must leave.'

'You can't!' She was horrified. 'Where would you go? You need to be here – for the vineyard!'

'There are other houses in Bellaise. I can find somewhere else.'

'You wouldn't be so cruel!' Her lips parted in dismay.

For a moment she thought he was going to defy her, and then he rested his hands on the mantel above the fire and pressed his forehead against its edge. 'No,' he agreed defeatedly. 'No, I could not go elsewhere in Bellaise, you are right. If I go, it must be away from here altogether.'

'But you can't. My father—'

He turned sideways to look at her. 'Your father – yes.

He has a lot to answer for, does he not?' He paused, and she found herself holding her breath for his answer. 'Very well, I will stay – at least for the present. Things will go on as before. But I warn you, if this does not work out I will have to make other arrangements.'

'What – other arrangements?'

He shrugged. 'A manager could run this place for you.'

'But it's your ability which has made it successful, it's your life!'

He turned to stare into the fire again. 'Yes. My life,' he muttered heavily. 'How many lives can a man have?'

Ryan didn't understand him. All she did understand was that for the present she had won a small respite. It was up to her now to see that she did nothing to destroy the tenuous thread that was keeping them together.

CHAPTER TEN

Two weeks later Ryan had another letter from Louise Ferrier.

A feeling of guilt possessed her when she read how disappointed Madame Ferrier had been not to receive a reply to her other letter, and how she hoped that Ryan was settling down to a happy marriage. She again renewed her invitation to both Ryan and Alain to visit her in Paris, but this time Ryan did not broach the subject with Alain.

Since that terrible evening when he had asked her to leave their relationship had deteriorated. To Ryan, who had dreamed of making their marriage a real one at last, the situation was very hard to bear, and only her love for him prevented her from making the break. She lived on her nerves when he was around and sometimes she wondered whether this self-inflicted torture was any worse than living apart from him would be. But to seriously consider a life without any part of him filled her with despair.

For Alain himself the situation was passably better, she thought. He was not plagued by emotion, and as he was out of the house most of the time, other matters filled his days. There was plenty to do about the vineyard – soil to be trenched and fertilized, new vines to be planted, established vines to be pruned and trained to the lowest wires of the cordons on which they would run.

Nevertheless, she was not unaware of the tensions in the household, no one could be, and Marie found it very difficult to curb her natural curiosity. She sensed that in some way the situation had changed, but she didn't know how and Ryan had no intention of enlightening her.

She had seen nothing more of David Howard, and one

day Marie confided that she had heard that Monsieur Alain had asked him not to visit the house again when he was not at home. This news had briefly lifted Ryan's spirits until she realized that Alain was not concerned about her, only about what other people might think. He didn't seem to care what they thought of his behaviour, but he seemed determined to prevent any speculation regarding Ryan's association with the young Englishman. For several days this knowledge irritated her, and she went out of her way to be awkward over the design and timing of his meals in an effort to arouse some comment, protesting or otherwise. But Alain merely disregarded her childishness and spent the waiting periods working in his study.

Ryan was beginning to wonder how long this could go on – how long before her nerves gave out completely – when she discovered something which brought everything into shocking focus.

To begin with, she hardly noticed it, that faint queasiness in the mornings and a sudden aversion to tea and coffee. She was so wrapped up in other considerations that the simple mechanics of her own body meant little to her until one morning when she was violently sick and a hasty calculation on her fingers revealed that certain functions were long overdue. Trembling, she sought the medical dictionary that she had once seen in the study, and by the means of elementary arithmetic worked out that she could be almost two months pregnant.

This revelation was so shattering that she spent the rest of the day staring unbelievingly into space, wondering desperately what she was going to do about it. Various methods of aborting the child crossed her troubled mind, but deep inside her she knew she would never deliberately do such a thing, whatever the circumstances. It wasn't so much the actual thought of abortion and what it might mean, as the awareness that she wanted Alain's child more than anything else in the world – except perhaps

Alain himself. It would be something of him that she could hold and care for and love, something that no one could take away from her.

But it was that very knowledge which troubled her most. This marriage could not support a child. Alain remained with her because of the vineyard. He would like for her to go. How could she confront him with the news that he was about to become a father? How could she have a child here and bring it up when its own father would despise what it stood for?

By the time Alain came home she was no more decided, and for once there was no sign of dinner cooking on the stove, the fire needed wood, and the house felt cold and uncared-for.

He came in and assessed the situation at once. Ryan was sitting at the table, the half empty cup of coffee she had made herself earlier cooling between her fingers. He regarded her pale face steadily for a moment, and then without a word bent to fling some logs on to the fire. When the flames were beginning to lick around the bark, he filled the kettle and set it to boil on the stove. Then he looked again at Ryan.

'What is the matter?' he asked. 'Are you ill?'

Ryan had decided in those few moments that illness was the safest answer. 'I – I haven't felt well all day,' she replied. That at least was the truth.

Alain frowned, and she flinched as he touched her forehead. 'You're not hot. How do you feel now?'

Ryan shrugged, finishing her coffee. 'I – I'm all right. Er – what do you want for dinner? Would omelettes and salad do?'

Alain pressed her back into the chair as she would have risen. 'Stay where you are,' he directed. 'I can manage. Are you hungry? Or don't you feel like eating?'

Ryan licked her lips. Truth to tell, she felt ravenous, and the idea of food was appealing. 'I – I am rather hungry,' she admitted. 'Perhaps I would feel better if I wasn't so – empty.'

Alain inclined his head. 'Very well. What would you like for dinner? Soup? Omelettes?' He opened the door of the refrigerator. 'Some fruit pie and cream?'

Ryan found a smile touching her lips, but it was such a relief to be talking to him again, even if it was to be short lived. 'A-all of those,' she conceded wryly, and he raised his eyebrows.

'All of them? Do you mean together?'

She smiled then. 'No, of course not. You know what I mean. Shall I help?'

He shook his head, rolling back the sleeves of his sweater. 'I am capable of making quite a passable omelette,' he replied, 'and I can open a tin of soup as well as you can.'

The meal was excellent, although the greater part of Ryan's enjoyment hinged on Alain's relaxed attitude. It was as though her supposed illness had made him aware of how much he relied upon her, and he talked quite companionably throughout the meal about the vineyard and the problems they would have to face when the grapes began to appear. There seemed to be so many disease preventive treatments needed throughout the summer months and Ryan marvelled that anyone could find the amount of work involved worthwhile. But Alain obviously did, and a little of his enthusiasm rubbed off on to her. And then she realized that come August and September, come the vintage, she would not be here, not in her condition. By her estimation the baby would be born in September, and by then she would have to have established a home for herself elsewhere.

Alain noticed the way her face suddenly changed, and with acute perception said: 'What is it? What is wrong? You've turned quite pale. You're not feeling ill again, are you?'

Ryan shook her head, getting to her feet. 'No. No, I just feel – tired, that's all.'

Alain rose too, and came round the table to her side, looking down at her rather doubtfully. 'Are you sure you feel all right?' he insisted, and she nodded vigorously.

'I'm just – tired. I've told you.'

'Why? What have you been doing? Marie is supposed to do all the heavy work.'

'She does.' Ryan moved her shoulders helplessly. 'I expect I didn't sleep too well last night.'

Alain pressed his lips together. 'Why not? You've not been troubled by that mouse again, have you?'

'No. Marie caught one in the kitchen a couple of weeks ago. I expect that was it.'

Alain nodded. Then almost against his will, he slid a hand under the weight of her hair and cupped her neck. 'You are very tense, are you not?' he asked, in a low voice, feeling the taut muscles at her nape. 'Has it been so terrible?'

'W-what?' she stammered.

'The situation.' He sighed 'I expect you think I have treated you abominably. I am sorry.'

She caught her breath. Was he apologizing? 'What do you mean?' she managed jerkily.

'I have been very selfish, thinking only of my own discomfort in this matter. I have never once considered how you must be feeling. It was a rude awakening, was it not?'

Ryan stirred beneath his fingers. 'I – I don't—'

'Be still!' His fingers tightened for a moment. 'Ryan, I have thought about this long and seriously, and I realize I was – hasty to ask you to leave. What am I, I ask myself, a man – or an animal? Must I always behave as the barbarian you once thought me?' He shook his head, and his mouth was thinner than a few moments ago. 'We are married. The good Abbé would be horrified if anything desecrated that contract, and I, as a good Catholic, must accept the bonds placed upon me. Therefore I suggest we attempt to salvage something from the wreck – attempt

155

to resume that somewhat tenuous relationship that at least satisfied the proprieties—'

Ryan jerked herself away from him then, her eyes glittering with unshed tears. For a few heart-stopping moments she had imagined he was about to ask her to share his bed, and the disappointment, combined with her own shuddering misery, was sufficient to drive her over the brink of good sense.

'What's the matter, Alain?' she taunted him unsteadily. 'Have you made your confession to the Abbé this morning, and has he told you that the way you are behaving is cold and inhuman? What did you say, I wonder? Forgive me, Father, for I have sinned? I seduced my wife, and when she tried to forgive me I told her to get out? Yes, that sounds reasonable. And what else? Let me see – I don't speak to my wife at all unless she asks a question to do with my laundry or my food or the housekeeping. Is that what you said? And did he absolve you? Am I to receive your compassion as a kind of penance for your misdemeanours—'

'*Be silent!*' Alain's voice was harsh and forbidding. 'How dare you speak to me like that?'

'Oh, I dare – I dare all sorts of things.' Ryan forced back the hot tears. 'My God, the arrogance of the man! To suggest that we resume a relationship that satisfies the proprieties! Whose proprieties? Yours – or mine? And since when have you cared about such things?'

'*Ryan*, you tempt me to demonstrate that I am your husband and therefore demand your respect!' he said explosively.

'Really! And how do you propose to accomplish that?'

'There – are – ways!' he retorted, unbuckling his belt, and fear like a bullet shot through her.

'You – you wouldn't – you wouldn't dare—' she began, but his face warned her that he might.

With a gasp of horror, she spun on her heel and fled

across the room and up the stairs as fast as her legs would carry her, not stopping until her bedroom door was behind her. She looked round desperately for something to secure the door, and suddenly realized that the thumping she had thought was the sound of him following her was only her heart, pounding violently in her chest. Nevertheless, she found a chair and secured it beneath the handle, accepting that it was merely a salutory defence. Nothing would keep Alain out if he chose to come in.

It was more than half an hour later that she heard him coming upstairs and presently there was a tap at her door. 'Are you asleep, Ryan?' he asked.

He paused, obviously waiting for her to answer, and when she did not, he went on heavily: 'I would not have beaten you, you know. God, you force me to do things I would have believed myself incapable of!'

Still she said nothing, and she heard, with a tremor of anticipation, his impatient ejaculation. Then he said: 'Very well, Ryan, pretend to be asleep. But remember, there is always tomorrow!' And with that parting threat, he went away.

Ryan felt no fear after he had gone. She knew he would not force his way into her bedroom, but a deep depression was settling over her now that the thrill of the chase had subsided. She was in an impossible situation, more impossible than even he could imagine. In other circumstances, she might have taken his offer of friendship on its face value. Now, she could not. Friendship was something she and Alain could never share, and she shrank from the pity which might be hers if he discovered she was expecting a baby. She did not want him on those terms. If all he could offer was friendship for appearances' sake, there was no future for either of them.

By the time she had crept along to the bathroom and had a wash, returned and undressed and crawled into bed she had come to a decision. She would go away – but not back to England. At least, not immediately. First, she would leave this district, find herself rooms in some anonymous city, and then write to Alain for some money. From a distance her demands would seem cold and reasonable, and no doubt Alain would be relieved to be rid of his unwanted responsibilities. It was what he had wanted, after all, and there was no reason why he should ever learn the truth behind her departure.

But where should she go? Unwillingly, thoughts of Louise Ferrier drifted into her mind. She was tempted to write to her and ask whether she might accept her invitation. But letters took time, and apart from the fact that too many people passed her letters through their hands, she had no reason to suppose that Louise would answer her when she had not replied to either of her missives. No, if she was to go and see Louise Ferrier, it would have to be an unheralded visit.

She tossed and turned restlessly beneath the covers of the bed. Could she throw herself on her father's aunt like that? Could she go to Paris without warning the old lady of her intentions? And why should she want to? She had told Alain that she wasn't a child, and yet here she was thinking like one.

But it was useless berating herself. Right now, she needed someone who cared about her, someone to talk to, someone to share the anxieties she was suffering. Louise was at least a member of the family. She would know what to do for the best. Ryan had no idea what arrangements there were in France for mothers with babies, but Louise might. And if she didn't, she would know how to find out.

She rolled on to her stomach and buried her face in the pillow. She could write to Alain from Paris, and once he had sent her some money she could see about getting an apartment of her own. She very much doubted whether Alain would even recognize Louise's address on her letter, and if he didn't, so much the better. Even if he did, she did not think he would follow her there. As he had said, he only knew *of* the woman, and she was not a relative of his, after all.

The decision was made. Tomorrow Ryan would have to see about getting into Anciens, and from there she could catch a train for the capital. She need only take the minimum necessities with her. She could send for her other things once she was settled. She knew that she should tell Alain of her decision, but somehow she couldn't. She was very much afraid that if she told him she was going she would break down and confess her reasons, and that would defeat everything. Her best plan was to leave while he was out at the vineyard. She would leave him a note, so he would not worry, and then write to him once she had reached her destination . . .

Louise Ferrier's house was in a suburb of Paris. It was a rather elegant suburb, and Ryan, who had been expecting something like the house her aunt used to live in, was shocked when the cab halted at the foot of stone steps leading up to a tall, graceful town house. The house was set in a square of such houses, with a central park surrounded by iron railings. All the houses in the square looked charming and well cared for, and white shutters and wrought iron balconies gave an air of refinement and gracious living.

Ryan looked hastily at the letter heading in her hand and then leaning forward to the cab driver said: 'Are you sure this is the place?'

The cab driver smiled round at her. In her jeans and fur-trimmed coat, her hair tumbled about her face after her sleepless night on the train, she was inordinately attractive, and he wondered what was bringing her here, to St. Hélène, at this hour of the morning.

'This is the place, *mademoiselle*,' he nodded firmly. 'Number twenty-two, *n'est-ce pas?*'

Ryan sighed, still not convinced, but she slid obediently

out of the cab and rummaged in her handbag to find the francs to pay him. Then, after he had rattled away across the cobbled stones, she picked up her suitcase and mounted the steps to the door. She glanced at her watch.

It was barely eight-thirty. Would anyone be about at this time? But she had received so many curious glances at the station that in desperation she had hailed a cab and arrived here at least an hour before she had intended.

There was a bell-pull and she tugged it, hearing the chimes echo throughout the house. Curtains still covered the upstairs windows and their thickness was eloquent of the opulence within.

A black-clad maid wearing a white cap and apron answered her ring and stood looking at her expectantly: '*Oui, mademoiselle*?'

'*Madame*,' corrected Ryan automatically, and then speaking in French, she said: 'I – er – is Madame Ferrier at home?'

The maid frowned and for a minute Ryan was convinced she had come to the wrong place. The hall behind the maid was thickly carpeted in blue and gold, the walls were panelled, and there was a fan-shaped staircase, also carpeted, winding to the upper floors. This couldn't be the home of her father's aunt. It simply couldn't!

'Who shall I say is calling – *madame*?' The faint hesitation in pronouncing her designation was doubtful.

Ryan took a deep breath. 'I have come to the right place then? This is the home of Madame Ferrier? Madame – *Louise* Ferrier?'

'Yes, *madem – madame*!'

There was a sound behind the maid and another woman appeared. For a brief moment Ryan thought this might be her great-aunt, but the long black gown and air of command spoke more of a housekeeper. How many servants did Louise Ferrier have?

'What is going on here, Colette?' The older woman spoke brusquely. 'Are you having difficulties?'

Ryan took a step forward on to the threshold. 'I – I have come to see my – aunt, *madame*. I am – Ryan – Ferrier.'

She said Ferrier deliberately, and the woman frowned. 'You are the young woman who has married Monsieur Alain?' she exclaimed in astonishment.

Ryan would scarcely have expected to be described thus in her aunt's house, but she nodded and said: 'Yes. My name is de Beaunes now. I was Ryan Ferrier before I got married.'

The older woman shook her head in amazement. Then she gathered her composure. 'Well, you had better come in, *mademoiselle*.' She smiled as Ryan picked up her suit-case and carried it on to the blue and gold piling of the carpet. 'I am sorry, I should say *madame*, of course. But you look so young.'

Ryan didn't feel very young. She was feeling deathly tired and the morning sickness which up until now had been diverted by other discomforts now returned to cause her to sway unsteadily, and say: 'Do you think – oh, please, where is the bathroom?'

The woman hastily opened a door to one side of the hall and showed her into a small but exquisitely furnished cloakroom. There was a pale green toilet and handbasin, and the taps, and the mirror which reflected her strained face, were gilt-edged and polished.

By the time Ryan emerged feeling slightly faint, her suitcase had disappeared, and so, too, had the young maid. The elder woman still stood there, and regarded her with some concern.

'You are better now, *mademoiselle*?' she queried gently, and Ryan nodded. 'Very good. Now I will introduce myself. I am Madame Lefevre, the housekeeper to your aunt, Madame Ferrier. Your aunt has been informed of your arrival, and as soon as you feel up to it I am to take you to her.'

Ryan was taking deep breaths and beginning to feel a

little more human. But she was hungry now, and she wondered if she might ask for a drink of water before coping with anything else.

As though able to read her thoughts, Madame Lefevre added, 'If there is anything else you would like, *madame* ... Some coffee, perhaps, or something to eat ...'

'I – I would like a drink of water,' murmured Ryan awkwardly.

'Water?' Madame Lefevre was clearly surprised. Then her expression changed, and she smiled. 'But of course. Please – follow me.'

Ryan left her coat in the hall and followed the house-keeper into a bright sunlit room overlooking the walled garden at the back of the house. A circular dining table was laid with a white cloth, but there was no evidence that anyone had eaten there.

'If you will wait here, I shall not be a moment,' essayed Madame Lefevre, and with another encouraging smile she left her.

Ryan was glad to sink down on to one of the dining chairs and rest her aching body. It seemed days, not just hours, since she had been able to relax, and weariness enveloped her like a shroud. She wondered briefly whether Alain had found her note and then decided that he would have done. She had left it in a prominent place. She only hoped that David had been able to return the Land-Rover without being observed.

Getting into Anciens had not been easy. There was no taxi service in Bellaise, and besides asking anyone from the village would have aroused acute speculation. David had been her only hope, and he had come to her assistance without demur. She knew he saw helping her as a way of getting his own back on Alain for the way he had treated him, but it had been her only avenue of escape.

Yesterday morning she had stayed in bed late, waiting until Alain had left the house before venturing downstairs. Then, after Marie had arrived, she had left her to go down to the village, ostensibly to collect some stores. She had found David at the school and told him what she wanted to do. Naturally she had not gone into her reasons, but Alain's attitude towards her had convinced the Englishman that she was leaving him because she was unhappy and nothing else.

She told him that there was a Land-Rover in the barn which Alain seldom used, but she couldn't drive. Alain had promised to teach her, but no doubt he was waiting for the spring. She couldn't wait that long.

Of course, David could drive, and that afternoon, after Marie had left, he came up to the house and collected her and her few belongings and drove her the twenty kilometres into Anciens. He had wanted to wait and see her safely on the train, but she had been afraid Alain would return to the house and find her and the Land-Rover missing, so he had left her and she had managed to get a seat on the night train. It had not been a comfortable journey. Had she sufficient money she might have been able to book a sleeper, but what little she had would barely see her to her aunt's house, and she did not want to have to borrow money to begin her new life.

She had arrived in Paris in the early morning and intended to wait in the restaurant at the station until much later. But she was here now, and for better or worse, she had committed herself.

She looked round the room. A high moulded ceiling was supported by walls hung with cream silk, and the curtains at the tall windows were made of apricot brocade. A carpet of eastern design was laid squarely in the middle of the floor, and beyond its limits the boards were highly polished. There were cabinets containing silver and glassware, and an unused carved fireplace with an intricately woven screen. The room was obviously centrally heated by some hidden source, and Ryan realized that everything she had seen in this house so far bore witness to the fact that her father's aunt was a very wealthy woman. Why had Alain never told her this? Surely he must have known. She would never have come here had she imagined such surroundings. She felt like a beggar in the house of the princess.

Madame Lefevre returned with a tray on which reposed a basket of warm rolls, curls of butter in a china dish, and a jug of iced fruit juice. There was also the water Ryan had originally asked for.

'Oh, really,' she exclaimed, when the housekeeper set the silver tray before her. 'You shouldn't have gone to such trouble!'

'It was no trouble, *madame*. I think you are hungry, and the orange juice is freshly squeezed.'

The fruit juice was indeed more refreshing than mere water would have been, and Ryan attacked the rolls with zest. It was always the same, once she had recovered from the nausea, she felt perfectly well again. Only in this instance she was tired, and that made her dread the interview which was to come.

Madame Lefevre left her to eat her breakfast and returned as she was wiping her mouth with the napkin. 'It was good?' she asked, and Ryan nodded.

'Thank you, it was delicious.' She got to her feet. There was no point in delaying the inevitable. 'Will you take me to Madame Ferrier now?'

She accompanied Madame Lefevre up the shallow staircase to the first floor landing. Here a balcony overlooked the hall below, and beyond it halls forked to the other rooms. Madame Lefevre took the hall to the left and stopped before a pair of double white doors. She tapped lightly, and a voice called: 'Come in.'

Ryan was urged in an enormous sitting room with a high carved ceiling and lavender silk walls. There were some exquisite pieces of French period furniture mingling comfortably with less formal furnishings upon a cream patterned carpet which Ryan guessed might be Aubusson. But it was the woman seated on a striped chaise-

164

longue who focused Ryan's attention. Her father's aunt, Louise Ferrier.

When she saw Ryan she got immediately to her feet and came to greet her, kissing her warmly on both cheeks and then holding her at arm's length to look at her. 'Well, Ryan,' she said, speaking in accented English. 'Welcome to Paris.' Her glance flicked to the housekeeper. 'Thank you, Madame Lefevre. You can go.'

When the door had closed behind the housekeeper, Ryan drew an unsteady breath. If Louise Ferrier's house was much different from what she had expected, her father's aunt was even more so. Although she was clearly not a young woman, Ryan guessed that she was in her sixties, she was by no means the frail semi-invalid of Ryan's imagination. Louise Ferrier was in possession of all her faculties, and was as attractively elegant as her house. At this hour of the morning she was dressed in a pale blue linen suit which complemented the slightly bluish tinge to her immaculately coiffured hair, and there were several strings of what Ryan guessed might be real pearls around her slender throat. There were diamond rings on her fingers, too, and if all the jewellery she was wearing was real, it must be worth a veritable fortune. It made Ryan, in her tight-fitting jeans and scarlet shirt, feel totally inadequate.

'Now,' went on Louise, releasing one of her hands to draw her to a low hide-covered couch, 'this is an unexpected surprise. But one with which I am wholly in approval,' she added warmly.

'Thank you.' Ryan perched on the edge of the couch wishing she did not feel so uneasy. 'I – this is a beautiful house, isn't it?'

'Is it?' Louise regarded her steadily, and there was something vaguely familiar about that stare. 'But I'm sure you didn't come here to see me to discuss the merits of my house.'

Ryan forced a smile. 'No.' She hesitated. 'I suppose you

think this is a terrible cheek – me coming here, I mean.'

'A terrible cheek? What is this? Ah, I think I know. You mean you think I might object?'

'Yes.' Ryan sighed. 'I should have written to you.'

'There was no need.' Louise frowned. 'I gather you came alone.'

'Oh – oh, yes.' Ryan nodded. 'Do – do you mind?'

Louise shook her head. 'No.' She gave Ryan a curious smile. 'You'll stay, of course.'

Ryan nodded again. 'For – for a few days. If – if I may.'

'Stay as long as you like. My home is yours.' Louise pressed Ryan's arm encouragingly. Then: 'Madame Lefevre tells me you were unwell on your arrival.'

'Yes.' Ryan shifted uncomfortably. 'I – the journey must have upset me.'

'You travelled overnight?'

'Yes.'

'And Alain permitted this?' Louise sounded amazed.

Ryan hesitated, then before she could have second thoughts, she burst out: 'Alain didn't know. He – he doesn't know where I am.'

If she had expected some horrified reaction from Louise, she was mistaken. Instead she merely nodded her head comprehendingly, and said: 'Why?'

Ryan rested her elbows on her knees and buried her face in her hands. 'I've left him,' she mumbled.

'I see.' Louise digested this for a few moments. 'Why? Because you're pregnant?'

Ryan's head jerked up. 'How do you – that is, how—'

'My dear child, I have had some experience of morning sickness myself. And Madame Lefevre has had six children. It is not something you can hide in a house of women, Ryan.'

Ryan sank back against the silky soft upholstery. 'I should never have come here,' she sighed helplessly.

Now Louise frowned. 'Why not? I am not reproving

166

you, child!'

'I didn't know, you see,' Ryan went on, almost as though the other woman had not spoken, 'I imagined you to be like – like my aunt, who died just before I came to live with my father. I never imagined anyone – anywhere – like this!'

Louise shook her head. 'I do not understand. You are – disappointed?

Ryan dragged herself upright. 'Heavens, no, *madame*. Not disappointed.' She sighed. 'But had I known that you were – well, wealthy, I should never have come.'

'Why ever not?'

Ryan shrugged. 'I had some crazy idea that you might be able to help me, that you might know what I should do. What facilities are available for someone like me, with – with a baby and – no husband.'

'I can help you, Ryan—'

'No.' Ryan shook her head. 'I – I couldn't take anything from you, *madame*.' She couldn't bring herself to say 'aunt'. 'I – I have nothing to give you in return. The – the person I imagined you to be from your letters was entirely different. I thought you were a lonely old woman, forgive me – someone who might welcome some company, someone who needed help with the housework, the shopping ... Your letters did not do you justice, *madame*. I am sorry. I'll leave just as soon as I get some money from Alain—'

'What nonsense!' Louise looked at her impatiently. 'Surely the situation has improved, not deteriorated! All right, so I am a wealthy woman – what of it? If you knew the truth of it I am extremely lonely. I have nothing – no one. I have material possessions, yes. I do not deny that. Nor do I deny that these possessions give me pleasure. That would be foolish. But believe me, I would exchange them all for the love of one other human being.'

Ryan felt a sense of compassion. 'But there must be

people who care about you, *madame*!' she exclaimed.

'Tell me, who?'

Ryan floundered. 'I am sure Madame Lefevre—'

'Servants?' Louise shook her head. 'Madame Lefevre respects me, I am sure, but love does not enter into our relationship.'

Ryan made a helpless gesture. 'Surely – you have children, grandchildren, *madame*?' she ventured.

'I had a son,' conceded Louise quietly. 'Oh, yes, I had a son once. But he obviously cares nothing for his mother.'

Ryan felt an overwhelming sense of pity for her. Suddenly she was seeing the woman who had written those letters, and it was a humbling experience. 'And is – is your son still alive, *madame*?' she questioned, feeling she had to know about this man who neglected his mother so.

'Oh, yes.' Louise reached out and took one of Ryan's hands between both of hers. 'Yes, Ryan. My son is alive and well and living in Bellaise.' Then, as Ryan's face mirrored her incredulity, she went on: 'That is my grandchild you are carrying, my dear. Now do you see why I want you to stay with me?'

CHAPTER ELEVEN

Ryan's room overlooked the square at the front of the house. It was the most delightful room she had ever occupied, with lemon yellow walls, a fluffy white carpet, and a wide comfortable bed, spread with an apple green quilt. The furniture was modern and fitted, and her few possessions looked forlorn in the long unit with its sliding doors.

Now the wintry sun had moved round the house from the back and was filtering in through the blinds, but at this hour of the afternoon its strength had wilted. Lying there, warm and relaxed, between real silk sheets, Ryan wished she could view her future with less foreboding, but in spite of Louise Ferrier's kindness she felt terribly alone.

With a sigh she slid out of bed and walked to the window. Spreading the slats of the blind, she looked down into the square. Since that shattering conversation with Alain's mother that morning, she had slept for several hours, and at least physically exhaustion had left her. But as her body recovered strength, so too did her mind, and despair was like a tangible knot inside her. What was she going to do?

To begin with, the revelation of discovering that Louise Ferrier was not only her father's aunt but also Alain's mother had driven all other considerations from her mind. It explained so much – the things Alain had said during his delirium, his refusal to come to Paris . . . It had also left a lot unexplained, not least his reasons for keeping Louise's identity a secret. Louise herself had been only too willing to make explanations, and gradually the reasons for her son's estrangement became clear. It had made Ryan realize, however, that their marriage had been doomed from the start.

'Alain's father died when he was only a teenager,' she had told her. 'Needless to say, he was not your grandfather's brother. No, Simon, my first husband, was an industrialist. He made quite a lot of money out of technical machinery, computers, that sort of thing, and naturally he wanted Alain to follow in his footsteps. Unfortunately, Alain was still at university when he died, and unable to take over his father's position. Simon was killed in a plane crash, you see. No one could have guessed he would die so young.' She sighed. 'The company foundered. As luck would have it, Simon had bought shares for me in other companies and I remained solvent, but our company, Alain's father's company, was taken over by the Marron organization.'

Ryan frowned. 'That name – Marron – I've heard it before.'

Louise nodded. 'No doubt you have. If Alain ever mentioned his first wife to you, he will have told you that her name was Julia Marron.'

'Of course,' Ryan nodded. 'He did once tell me her name. But that was all.'

Louise's smile was bitter. 'I am not surprised. It was a disastrous marriage, from start to finish.' She pleated the folds of her skirt. 'And of course, I was to blame.'

'You?'

'Yes.' Louise paused. 'When Alain had completed his degree, I arranged for him to meet Julia Marron on every occasion. I had this idea, you see, and as we all moved in the same social circle, it was not difficult to throw the two young people together. Julia's father, Henri Marron, was much older than my husband, and he was the head of the Marron organization. Julia was his only offspring. Do you see the way my mind was working?'

Ryan nodded. 'You hoped Alain would eventually gain control of his father's company again.'

'Not only that, Ryan. I was ambitious. I saw him as the

chairman of the Marron organization.' She shook her head regretfully. 'I was a fool. So ambitious! And look what it brought me!' She pressed her lips together. 'But it is no use decrying the past. I did what I did, and I regretted it bitterly. Alain married Julia, with encouragement. I should have guessed it would never last. Julia was too – too frivolous, too fond of parties and buying clothes to interest a serious man like my son. But mothers will always interfere. Unfortunately in my case, it ended as disastrously as it had begun.'

Ryan wished there was something she could say to alleviate the other woman's pain, but there was nothing.

Louise heaved a sigh. 'They split up after a couple of years. Initially Alain remained with the organization, but gradually his interest began to dwindle. We were still friends – acquaintances – in those days. He told me he was unhappy remaining an employee of his ex-wife's family. But I insisted it was foolish of him to give it all up when at some future date he and Julia might get together again.' She hesitated, her face strained. 'It didn't happen like that. Julia began pursuing him again. It was as though his lack of interest in her aroused her desire for him.' She paused, controlling herself. 'There was a terrible row one evening. Julia had been drinking. She had started drinking soon after their marriage, and I know Alain despised her for it. This particular evening she had gone to his apartment and tried to seduce him.' Her lips twisted. 'Alain threw all the sordid details at me later, that's how I know so much. He turned her out. She got in her car, one of those fast sports models, drove recklessly away, and – and killed herself.'

'Oh, no!'

'Oh, yes.' Louise nodded slowly. 'Not deliberately, I don't think. Julia was too selfish for that. But indirectly, I suppose, she managed it. At any event, when Alain discovered what had happened he came here, to my house, in a terrible state. He accused me of being responsible for

171

the whole sorry mess. And – and I suppose I was. No—' this as Ryan tried to protest, 'no, my dear, I know I forced him into that marriage. He would never have married anyone like Julia, had I not been behind him, urging him on.' She sighed again. 'Afterwards, he disappeared for a time. I think he spent some time in Italy, and eventually, through his solicitors, I discovered he had joined a man called Pierre Ferrier in his vineyard. Your father, my dear.' She squeezed Ryan's hand.

'But how – how is your name—?'

Louise half smiled. 'I got to know Emile Ferrier quite by accident. He was not involved in the wine-growing business, but he did own several stores where the Ferrier wines were sold. Again, I interfered. I allowed Emile to take me out, to visit me here – all to gain news of my son. Letters evinced no replies, and I did not dare to visit Bellaise myself. Eventually Emile asked me to marry him, and because I was fond of him, I agreed. I think that was another black mark against me so far as Alain was concerned. He saw my marriage as a deliberate attempt to ingratiate myself with the Ferrier family. And I suppose it was. But it did no good.' She lifted her shoulders. 'Emile died several years ago, and now I am alone again.' She looked at Ryan and now Ryan could see why she had thought there was something familiar about that stare. Her eyes were Alain's eyes. 'When I discovered that Pierre was dead and you had married Alain, I could not resist one more attempt. When you didn't answer my letter I guessed that Alain had prevented you.'

'No. No, he didn't.' Now it was Ryan's turn to look discomfited. 'He said if I wanted to go to Paris, I should go.'

'But he would not come with you?'

'No.'

'And of course, he made no mention of the fact that I was his mother?'

'No.' Ryan sighed. 'Why didn't you?'

Louise grimaced. 'My dear, it took a great deal of courage to sit down and write to you at all. I was risking Alain coming here and denigrating my name still further. No – I thought my relationship to your father might interest you sufficiently to persuade Alain—'

'Me? Persuade Alain?' Ryan was incredulous.

Louise nodded. 'I guessed as much, of course. It was so soon – your marriage, I mean. So soon after Pierre's death. I guessed there was more to it than there appeared.'

'My father left us each a half share in the vineyard, contingent upon us marrying one another.'

'Oh, no!' Louise stared at her. 'Poor Alain! So he has had two marriages thrust upon him!'

Until then this had not occurred to Ryan, but when it did it was a devastating realization.

Linking her fingers together, she said: 'You must understand, though, I never asked Alain to marry me. I didn't want to marry him. Not at first. I – I hated him. I knew nothing about him, you see, and I imagined he had taken advantage of my father. It was only later that I discovered that without him my father would have been ruined. His health was so bad, you see.' She swallowed convulsively. 'It – it was to be a marriage of convenience. And – and it worked. At first.'

Louise frowned. 'Then what happened?' she asked gently. 'Did Alain – take advantage of you?'

Ryan could have laughed had it not all been so serious. 'Oh, no,' she denied unsteadily. 'Alain was not to blame. I – I fell in love with him, you see, and – and I began – I began—'

' – wanting him?' Louise was astute. 'Oh, don't look so embarrassed, my dear. I know what it is like to want a man. I loved Simon very dearly, and when he was killed I was shattered.' She paused. 'Go on.'

Ryan moved her shoulders awkwardly. 'The inevitable happened. It wasn't Alain's fault. I – I asked for it. Afterwards, he was furious. He – he asked me to leave and go back to England.'

Louise shook her head. 'And you refused?'

'Yes.' Ryan caught her breath on a sob. 'I didn't want to leave him. I loved him. Just being near him was enough.'

Louise nodded understandingly, putting an arm about her shoulders. 'Don't go on. I can guess the rest. When you found you were expecting a baby, you were afraid of what he might say.' She gave a short mirthless laugh. 'I know the feeling.'

'I – I couldn't bear for him to feel – sorry for me.'

Louise held her closer. 'You poor child!' She sighed. 'And Alain doesn't know where you are?'

'No one knows. Oh – unless he gets anything out of David.'

'David?' Louise drew back to look at her. 'Who is David?'

'David Howard, an Englishman. He came to teach at the village school just after Christmas.'

'I see. This Englishman – he is a friend of yours?'

'You might say that. It – it was through him—' She broke off. 'He drove me into Anciens yesterday so that I could catch the night train to Paris.'

Louise's eyebrows ascended. 'You started to say something else. What was it?'

Ryan flushed. 'Nothing really. ' She sighed. 'Oh, well, I think Alain was – he didn't like for me to be friendly with David.'

'No?'

'No. He came back one afternoon unexpectedly, and found us talking together in the kitchen. He was furious!' She hunched her shoulders. 'That – that was the night . . .'

Louise gave her a curious look. 'Was it indeed? It seems to me that my son is not as blameless as you would have me believe.' She shook her head. 'But enough of that now. We can talk later. I suggest Madame Lefevre shows you to the room she is preparing for you and you rest for a while. Things always look brighter when one is not fatigued.'

And so Ryan had been shown to this delightful room with its equally delightful adjoining bathroom. She had showered the grime from her body and taking Alain's example had slid naked between the sheets.

Now she turned to the long mirror that was set in the wardrobe door and surveyed her naked body without pleasure. Her breasts were firm and filling out now, her waist narrow, her hips curved and unknowingly provocative, her legs long and slender. There was no sign yet that within the supple skin Alain's seed was strong and vital, no sign of the swelling life growing inside her. But in a few weeks her waistline would begin to thicken, and in a few months she would be big and clumsy. How could she have stayed at Bellaise, she demanded silently, longing to justify her actions? How could she have stayed with Alain knowing that every time he looked at her he was reminded of her foolishness and sickened by it?

With a sigh she thrust back the wardrobe door and took down the shirt and jeans she had worn earlier and which Madame Lefevre had put away for her. Then she put on her underwear, donned the shirt and jeans and brushed vigorously at her hair.

She was wondering where she might find her aunt when there was a knock at her bedroom door. Quickly she pulled it open and stood back to allow the maid, Colette, to enter with a tray.

'Madame Lefevre sent a small snack, *madame*,' she explained politely, setting the tray on the table by the window. 'Dinner is not until later and she thought you might be hungry after your rest.'

Ryan's mouth twitched. 'That was kind of her,' she exclaimed, touched by the housekeeper's thoughtfulness which no doubt had been instigated by Louise Ferrier. 'Thank you.'

Colette departed and Ryan examined the tray. There was a dish of cold consommé, something which would not have spoiled had she still been asleep, some rolls, and a fluffy peach mousse to finish with. A glass of fruit juice accompanied the meal, and Ryan drank this thirstily.

Colette returned just as she was finishing and smiled at the empty dishes. 'You are feeling better now, *madame*?' she suggested, and Ryan nodded. 'That is good. Madame Ferrier is in the sitting room. If you would like to join her, I will show you the way.'

Louise Ferrier smiled and rose to her feet when Ryan came into the room. 'Ah, you look much better, my dear,' she exclaimed with satisfaction. 'Are you feeling rested?'

'Very much.' Ryan forced a smile. 'And I've just had the most delicious snack!'

'Ah!' Louise nodded. 'So – sit down!' and when Ryan was seated: 'Did you bring any other clothes with you?'

Ryan grimaced at her jeans. 'You mean instead of these? Just a skirt and a couple of sweaters, I'm afraid.'

Louise considered her thoughtfully. 'You would pay for dressing, my dear. Did anyone ever tell you, you're quite beautiful, you know?'

Ryan couldn't help colouring. 'You're very kind.'

'Not kind. Just truthful.' Louise spread her hands. 'We must see about getting you some new clothes. I shall enjoy that.'

'Oh, but—'

'No buts, my dear. I insist. You simply cannot stay here with me, meet my friends, wearing jeans and a sweater, no matter how casual today's fashions may be. Besides, this is what we have to talk about, is it not? Your staying here?'

Ryan curved her arms round her knees, curling her body into a hunched position. 'You know I can't stay here. Not now.'

'Why not?' Louise stared at her.

'Well – because you're Alain's mother, for one thing.'

'You think that is a good reason for leaving?' Louise's voice was low and taut, and Ryan felt contrite.

'Oh, please, try to understand. If – if he finds out I am here, he will think I am – taking advantage of your good nature.'

Louise snorted. 'If my son finds you here, he is much more likely to think exactly the opposite. You forget, Alain and I . . .' She broke off. 'But this is silly. Of course you will stay here. This is your home. Not only are you my great-niece, but also my daughter-in-law. Where else would a daughter go than to her mother at a time like this?'

Ryan was moved by her kindness. 'But how can you introduce me to your friends?' she exclaimed. 'I'm pregnant, remember? In a few months I shall look ghastly!'

Louise chuckled. 'In a few months you will look even more beautiful than you do at the moment. We'll buy some of those long high-waisted maternity dresses, and you'll look marvellous! Don't you know that a woman's skin and hair – her complexion – everything acquires a glow during pregnancy?'

'Alain said he liked me in long dresses,' Ryan murmured, almost involuntarily, and Louise regarded her gently.

'We'll have to let Alain know where you are, you realize that, don't you?' she said quietly.

'*No!*' Ryan jerked upright. 'I mean – why?' She moved her shoulders helplessly. 'I was thinking I could write to him care of a box number—'

Now it was Louise's turn to say no. 'It wouldn't be fair, or wise,' she said. 'After all, if everything you say is true, Alain won't come here. He won't risk seeing me again just to make monetary arrangements with you. We'll write and tell him where you are in a day or so, it won't hurt him to wait that long, and no doubt he'll be only too glad to know you're at least in decent surroundings. If you don't give him an address to write to, curiosity may do what satisfaction won't.'

Ryan could see the logic of the argument, but she wasn't happy about it. 'And – the baby?'

Louise looked thoughtful. 'I don't know. That's up to you, of course. You want to keep it, don't you?'

'Oh, yes!' Ryan was vehement.

Louise smiled. 'I knew you would. As for Alain – I don't know. I suppose sooner or later he must be told.' Then at Ryan's drawn expression, she sighed. 'We can discuss that later. For the present, it is sufficient that you are here.'

During the evening, over a delicious meal served by Madame Lefevre, Ryan managed to relax a little. Although she was still far from convinced that she should stay here, she was prepared to accept that for a few days she had no decisions to make. Louise was lonely, she bitterly regretted the past, and Ryan guessed that by having her son's wife here, albeit his estranged wife, she felt nearer to her son. Nine years was a long sentence for anyone to serve, and she wished there was something she could do to help the unhappy woman. Then she chided herself derisively. She was helpless; she could not even help herself.

Because Ryan had slept during the afternoon and Louise was eager to hear everything about her life in England and her subsequent marriage, it was late when they went to bed. Even so, Ryan did not feel sleepy. Talking about Alain had brought his presence into the room, and she found herself wondering how he had coped this first day on his own. No doubt Marie had been there to help him. She would hardly be able to contain her curiosity. And Alain himself? Would he feel curious or anxious about her? Or would he breathe a sigh of relief because she had gone?

Louise had lent her a nightdress. It was a froth of pale green lace that tied at the neck with satin ribbons. It was

178

the most feminine item Ryan had ever worn, and as she sat at the vanity unit brushing her hair she thought how ironic it was that she should be wearing something so delicate when only she would see it. She sighed. Was it true? Did women acquire an added allure when they were pregnant? She would hardly have thought so, contemplating how shapeless they became. She supposed rather sadly that a man who loved his wife might feel a sense of pride of possession, but that was all. But for her there would be no such satisfaction.

Thrusting the brush aside, she switched out all the lights and walked to the window. The street lights illuminated the square below, cold and shadowy in the darkness. But even as she watched, a cab drew into the square and she thought inconsequentially that others than themselves kept late hours in St. Hélène.

The cab rattled over the cobbles, coming right round the square to stop outside Louise Ferrier's house. Ryan's eyes widened. Surely Louise was expecting no visitors at this time of night? A man thrust open the door of the cab and climbed out – a big man, wearing a dark overcoat, whose silvery fair hair glinted in the lamplight. Ryan looked – and then looked again. She shook her head. No! She was imagining things. The man down in the square was nothing like Alain. He was someone coming to the house next door, and her sensitized emotions were painting Alain's image on a complete stranger.

The door bell jangled noisily, and Ryan fell back against the wall of her bedroom. The bell rang again, and she put her hands over her ears. It couldn't be Alain, it just couldn't! And if it was – what did he want? What was he doing coming to his mother's house when for nine years he had stayed away?

She went to the door of her room and opened it silently. Someone was going downstairs to answer the door. She guessed it would be Louise. Madame Lefevre and Colette had retired several hours ago. She peered at her wrist watch on the bedside table. It was half past two. What in heaven's name was Alain doing?

Downstairs, the door was opened and there was a swift interchange of voices.

'*Alain!*'

'Hello, Mother.'

'But what are you doing here?'

'Is Ryan here?'

Silence. Then: 'Don't you think you'd better tell me what is going on? Why should – Ryan be here?'

The door closed. 'For heaven's sake, Mother, if she is here, *tell me*!'

'Yes. Yes, as a matter of fact, she is.'

'Oh, thank God!' There was an overwhelming sense of relief in his words. 'Where is she? I want to see her.'

'At this time of night? Alain—' His mother's words were a protest, but Ryan could hear her husband mounting the stairs and panic broke out all over her. She swiftly closed the bedroom door, and hurried to the bed, sliding between the sheets and closing her eyes. But her heart was beating rapidly and anyone hearing her quickened breathing would know immediately that she was shamming.

'Which room did you put her in?' She could hear Alain's voice outside, and his mother saying:

'Alain, are you out of your mind? Ryan will be asleep. Don't you think you've done enough to that poor child?'

'Which room?' Alain was opening doors and Ryan could have told Louise that she was wasting her time. He reached her door and opened it, switching on a lamp. Ryan's eyes opened and he stared into them, and then nodded heavily. 'This one.' He turned to his mother. 'You don't mind if I stay, I suppose?'

Louise, holding her silk wrapper closely about her, looked helplessly at Ryan. 'My dear, what do you want me to do?'

Ryan propped herself up on one elbow, but before she could reply, Alain interposed: 'Just leave us alone for a while, Mother, please. I want to talk to Ryan.'

'But couldn't it have waited until morning—' his mother began, and Alain uttered an impatient expletive.

'Till morning?' he echoed. 'My God, have you any idea what kind of day I've had? What kind of night I had last night? You talk about waiting until the morning as if this were a social visit, instead of the end of a search to find my wife!'

Louise drew herself up to her full height. 'And why should you wish to find your wife, Alain?' she demanded. 'I understood you asked her to leave.'

Alain raked his fingers through his hair. 'I did. That's right, I did. But that was when—' He broke off. 'Mother, this is between Ryan and me. Let me finish it!'

'Ryan was most distressed when she arrived here,' persisted Louise steadily. 'Why should I assume that she wants to speak to you? She left you a note telling you she would write to you in a few days. Why couldn't you have waited? Why have you come here, persecuting the girl? What right have you to burst in here at this time of night and demand to speak to her?'

'Louise—'

Ryan felt bound to say something, but Alain was staring at his mother. 'My God, you want your pound of flesh, don't you?' he muttered. 'All right, you shall have it. I'm here because I love her, and I've been almost out of my mind since she disappeared! Does that answer your question?'

A faint twitching assailed Louise's lips. 'I see,' she murmured, not without some satisfaction, but Ryan was staring at Alain incredulously.

'Wh – what did you say?' she breathed, and Alain looked angrily at his mother.

'Now, will you leave us alone?' he demanded, and

Louise slowly nodded her head.

'If that's what Ryan wants,' she agreed.

Ryan was upright in the bed, the sheet drawn up to her chin, her eyes wide and disbelieving. But she nodded, and Louise gave a small sigh and withdrew.

After she had gone, Alain stood for a few moments staring at Ryan, and then he turned away and took off his overcoat. He tossed it carelessly on to the table by the window, and said: 'In God's name, Ryan, why did you do it?'

Ryan's voice, when she found it, was croaky and unsteady. 'I – I thought it was what you wanted.'

'Why?' He unbuttoned the jacket of the dark suede suit he had worn the day they got married. 'Because of what happened two nights ago? Did I frighten you? I didn't intend to. But you make me—' He broke off. 'Well?'

Ryan sighed. 'That was only incidental. I didn't leave you because I was afraid of you. I would have left you anyway.'

A spasm of pain crossed his face, and in the lamplight she could see how tired and and strained he was looking. 'I see. Had – was it to do with Howard?'

'Howard? You mean – David Howard?'

He took a menacing step towards her. 'Oh God, of course I mean David Howard!'

'No. No, of course not.'

'But he took you to Anciens, didn't he? He knew where you were going?'

'No.'

Patently he didn't believe her. 'Well, anyway, I think he got more than he bargained for,' he muttered with satisfaction.

'What do you mean?' Ryan was anxious now. 'How – how did you find out David took me into Anciens?'

'Because the Land-Rover broke down on his way back!' retorted Alain tightly. 'Have you any idea what I thought – what I imagined when I discovered not only you and the Land-Rover but also Howard had disappeared?'

Ryan licked her lips. 'Wh – what happened?'

Alain flung himself about the room. 'I got drunk – that's what happened. Very drunk! I don't know how much I consumed. It seemed to take a long time for anything to blunt the – the realization that you had gone!'

'Oh, Alain!' She stared at him helplessly. 'And – and David?'

Alain heaved a sigh. 'I was sure the pair of you had gone away together. When Howard brought the Land-Rover back in the early hours of yesterday morning, I nearly beat the living daylights out of him!'

'Oh, no!'

Alain shook his head. 'I was half out of my mind. Can you understand that? It was only when he managed to get out the word Couvrier that I realized he had got Gilles, Vivienne's stepson, out to tow him back.'

'Is – is he all right?'

Alain's lips twisted. 'I suspect he's got a broken nose, and no doubt a few bruises he didn't deserve, but he'll live.'

'And – and he told you where I had gone?'

'Not exactly, no. But I knew you had very little money, certainly not enough to go to England. I guessed you might come here.'

'To your mother's!'

'She told you? I guessed she would.'

'And why not? Oh, Alain, she's been so kind to me.'

'Has she?' Alain sounded strained. 'And do you intend to stay here?'

'To – stay – here?' Ryan moved her shoulders tremblingly.

Alain came to stand beside the bed, looking down at her. 'Well?' he said huskily. 'Do you?'

'Is – is that what you want me to do?'

Alain shook his head impatiently. 'Dear God, Ryan, I

have no rights where you are concerned. I forfeited them a couple of months ago.'

'When you made love to me?'

'When I – took your innocence,' he corrected her quietly.

Ryan put out a hand and stroked her fingers down his thigh. 'Why did you come here, Alain? Why didn't you wait until I wrote to you?'

Alain's jaw tightened, but he didn't stop her caressing fingers. 'I – I think we should get something straight,' he muttered unevenly. 'I had seen you before you came to Bellaise.'

Ryan's fingers closed round his leg. 'You had seen me? How?'

'I went to England – on your father's instructions – two years ago. I – went to the library where you were working, and I watched you for a while.'

'But why?'

'Your father was curious about you. Surely you guessed that. He wanted to know what you were like. I told him!'

Ryan shook her head. 'What are you trying to tell me?'

Alain looked down at her with eyes grown suddenly dark. 'I knew what your father planned to do, and I agreed.'

'To – to our marriage, you mean?'

'Yes, yes.' Alain raked his fingers through his hair again. 'Oh, I realize it was crazy – *crazy!* I was far too old for you, and besides, I knew nothing about you. But when you came to Bellaise, I fell in love with you, and I despised myself for doing so.'

'But – but why?'

'Ryan, I'm twenty years older than you are.' He sighed. 'Oh, I had it all mapped out in my mind. We were going to get married, and gradually, as you got older, I'd have shown you how I felt. But it didn't work that way. Everything you did made me aware of you, and because of this I hurt you, continually. I resented the way you made me feel.' He unloosened his tie and pulled it off. 'I had had one disastrous marriage, which no doubt my mother has told you about, and I didn't dare risk ruining our chances of happiness. But you became angry over Vivienne, and I was as jealous as hell over Howard! It was explosive, and it blew up, right in my face,'

'But you asked me to leave!'

'I know I did. What else could I do? I didn't know whether I would be able to leave you alone after – after that night . . .' He shook his head. 'I had some idea that if you went away for a while, grew up a bit, you might see me differently when I came to find you.'

'And – Vivienne?'

'What about Vivienne?' He scowled.

'Did – did she compensate you?'

Alain swore violently. 'No. No, of course she didn't – compensate me. All right—' he shrugged his broad shoulders, 'once I did spend a lot of time with her. But since that trip to England – since I got to know you – there have been no other women.' He bent his head. 'At least – not in the village.' He sighed. 'I'm not a celibate, you know. There have been times . . .'

Ryan was trembling so much, she could hardly sit still. 'And now?'

Alain shifted restlessly. 'That is up to you.'

'Do you want me to come back?'

Alain ran a hand round the back of his neck. 'Of course I do.' He hesitated. 'Ryan, could we try it again? Could we try and make it work?'

Ryan looked up at him for a moment, and then she slid deliberately out of bed, knowing what the sight of her slender body clad only in the lace gown would do to him. 'We might,' she essayed slowly. 'But things would have to be – different.'

'How different?' His eyes were narrowed.

Ryan turned to look at him steadily, her heart in her eyes. 'I should want to share everything with you,' she murmured. 'Including – your bed.'

Alain stared at her for a moment, and then with an exclamation he caught her in his arms, holding her closely against him so that she could feel every vibrant muscle leaping against hers. 'Do you know what you're saying?' he demanded thickly.

'I love you, Alain,' she whispered huskily, winding her bare arms round his neck. 'Now please – stop talking and make love to me . . .'

Hours later, Ryan awoke to find it was morning. For a few moments the events of the night before assumed a dreamlike unreality, and she dared not turn her head in case she found she was alone. But then she realized that a warm body was close to hers in the comfortable bed, and when she did turn to look she found Alain, sound asleep, beside her. He was lying on his back, and she couldn't resist the impulse to run her hands over his chest and stomach.

'Mmm,' he murmured lazily, opening his eyes and finding her regarding him. 'We don't have to get up yet, do we?'

Ryan half smiled. 'I don't know what your mother will say. She didn't expect you to come here. You'll have to talk to her.'

'Nothing would have kept me away,' he groaned, burying his face in the curve of her neck. 'But I agree, I will have to talk to her. But later – much later.'

Ryan sighed, realizing the moment of truth had come. 'Alain,' this as he began to caress her, 'Alain, I have something else to tell you.'

'Can't it wait?' he asked, kissing the corner of her mouth, and it was difficult to resist him in this mood.

'No,' she said firmly, forcing herself not to succumb. 'Alain – Alain, I'm going to have a baby!'

For a moment Alain was still, and then he propped himself up on one elbow and looked down at her, his eyes dark and disturbing. 'You are pregnant?'

Ryan nodded, half anxious at his possible reaction.

'Oh, Ryan!' He bent his head and kissed her urgently. 'Was this – was this why you left me?'

'I was afraid,' she stumbled. 'I was afraid you would hate me because I would remind you of – of what had happened!

'Oh, Ryan!' he said again, lowering himself down to her. 'What a fool I've been! Will you forgive me?'

'You're – you're not – angry?'

'Angry?' He gave a snort. 'Angry? I'm – delighted.' Then his eyes clouded. 'But are you?' He sighed frustratedly. 'You're so young! I should have waited—'

She spread her fingers over his lips to silence him. 'Don't be silly,' she exclaimed. 'I shall be twenty in two months. Quite old enough to have a husband and family.'

'And – my mother – knows this?'

Ryan nodded. 'She guessed. I – I've been rather unwell in the mornings.'

'But not this morning?' he asked, concern drawing his brows together.

'It doesn't happen until I get up,' she explained with a smile. Then: 'Your mother wanted me to stay here. She's so lonely, Alain. Can't you – couldn't you forget – the past?'

Alain stroked her cheek tenderly. 'The past was forgotten long ago. But people are proud; they avoid making apologies.' He smiled. 'But things are different now. You are here. The ice has been broken. Have no fear – I can afford to be generous now.'

Ryan had never known happiness could be like this, so wonderfully warming and ecstatic all at the same time. 'When will we go back to Bellaise?' she asked.

Alain stretched lazily. 'I don't know. Two – maybe

three days. We'll spend a couple of days with my mother now we're here.'

'I hoped you'd say that. And maybe – maybe when I have the baby, she could come and stay with us.'

'We'll see.' Alain was tolerant. 'I suppose I must apologize to Howard, too, although I still resent his interfering.'

Ryan chuckled, loving the way she could touch him without fear of rebuff. 'You ought to feel grateful to him,' she said teasingly. 'If he hadn't taken me to Anciens – if you hadn't come to find me – it might have been months before we discovered the truth.

Alain gave her a wry look. 'You think so?' he murmured. 'You think my son might not have made his presence known before then?'

And Ryan could not deny the truth of this. Come the vintage, she would still be at Bellaise.

Did you miss our splendid Doctor/Nurse Series?

Published earlier this year, three Double Volumes by three of your favourite authors:

Anne Hampson

UNWARY HEART

For her family's sake, Muriel had to find a rich husband—and she fixed on Andrew Burke. But Andrew was one jump ahead of her—or was he?

BEYOND THE SWEET WATERS

After her fiancé died, Jeanette had vowed never to marry—until she met Craig Fleming and changed her mind. But Craig, it seemed, was already bound to another woman.

Anne Mather

THE ARROGANT DUKE

Juliet had run away from her domineering father—but her new employer, the Duque Felipe Ricardo de Castro, was not only just as domineering, but she had managed to fall in love with him!

SWEET REVENGE

The imposing Conde Vincente della Maria Estrada was not the sort of man who was likely to take kindly to being deceived. And when Toni Morley tried to do just that he proceeded to exact a subtle revenge.

Violet Winspear

COURT OF THE VEILS

'The desert is like a woman ... But a man can enjoy the desert without getting involved — emotionally.' Duane Hunter's words made it plain to Roslyn that there was no future for her in his life. And yet ...

TENDER IS THE TYRANT

Maxim di Corte, director of a famous ballet company, would have no difficulty in making Lauri submit to him as a dancer—but could he make her submit to him as a woman?

50p net each

FREE!

Your copy of the Mills & Boon Catalogue —

'Happy Reading'

If you enjoyed reading this MILLS & BOON romance and would like to obtain details of other MILLS & BOON romances which are available, or if you are having difficulty in getting your TEN monthly paperbacks from your local bookshop, why not drop us a line and you will receive, by return and post free, the MILLS & BOON catalogue—'*Happy Reading*'.

Not only does it list nearly 400 MILLS & BOON romances, but it also features details of all future publications and special offers.

For those of you who can't wait to receive our catalogue we have listed over the page a selection of current titles. This list may include titles you have missed or had difficulty in obtaining from your usual stockist. Just tick your selection, fill in the coupon below and send the whole page to us with your remittance including postage and packing. We will despatch your order to you by return!

MILLS & BOON READER SERVICE, P.O. BOX 236, 14 Sanderstead Road, South Croydon, Surrey, CR2 0YG, England.

Please send me the free Mills & Boon catalogue ☐

Please send me the titles ticked ☐

I enclose £............................ (No. C.O.D.) Please add 5p per book—standard charge of 25p per order when you order five or more paperbacks. (15p per paperback if you live outside the U.K. & Europe).

Name.. Miss/Mrs

Address ....

City/Town ....

County/Country ....Postal/Zip Code...............

XP75

Your Mills & Boon Selection!

☐ 001
THE BLACK CAMERON
Jean S. MacLeod

☐ 002
MY TENDER FURY
Margaret Malcolm

☐ 003
LOVE IS FOR EVER
Barbara Rowan

☐ 004
WHO LOVES BELIEVES
Elizabeth Hoy

☐ 005
SECRET HEIRESS
Eleanor Farnes

☐ 006
GREENFINGERS FARM
Joyce Dingwell

☐ 007
THE THIRD UNCLE
Sara Seale

☐ 008
MARRY A STRANGER
Susan Barrie

☐ 104
THE GIRL AT WHITE DRIFT
Rosalind Brett

☐ 130
THE AFFAIR IN TANGIER
Kathryn Blair

☐ 132
RIVER NURSE
Joyce Dingwell

☐ 133
INHERIT MY HEART
Mary Burchell

☐ 156
A CASE OF HEART TROUBLE
Susan Barrie

☐ 253
MISS MIRANDA'S WALK
Betty Beaty

☐ 255
PARADISE ISLAND
Hilary Wilde

☐ 269
A PLACE CALLED PARADISE
Essie Summers

☐ 283
ISLE OF SONG
Hilary Wilde

☐ 287
THE PRIDE YOU TRAMPLED
Juliet Armstrong

☐ 288
WINTERSBRIDE
Sara Seale

☐ 293
HOTEL BY THE LOCH
Iris Danbury

☐ 298
QUEEN'S COUNSEL
Alex Stuart

☐ 300
HOTEL SOUTHERLY
Joyce Dingwell

☐ 302
BELOVED SPARROW
Henrietta Reid

☐ 304
THE MASTER OF
NORMANHURST
Margaret Malcolm

☐ 307
THE DREAM AND THE
DANCER
Eleanor Farnes

All priced at 25p net

Please tick the titles you require and use the handy order form overleaf for your requirements.